Sam in the Spotlight

Sam in the Spotlight

Anne-Marie Conway

USBORNE

For everyone at Full Circle –
my inspiration for the Star Makers series.
Miss you loads! x

First published in 2011 by Usborne Publishing Ltd., Usborne House,
83-85 Saffron Hill, London EC1N 8RT, England.
www.usborne.com

A CIP catalogue record for this book is available from the British Library.

FMAMJJASOND/11 02152/1 ISBN 9781409521419
Printed in Reading, Berkshire, UK.

I am Sam... Sam I am!

My favourite book ever when I was a little girl was *Green Eggs and Ham* by Dr. Seuss. Not because I like weird food or anything, but because of the opening lines: I *am Sam. Sam I am.* I bet I thought Dr. Seuss had written it just for me! My big sister Crystal used to read it to me over and over until I knew every word by heart. We would cuddle up together on my bed, with my beautiful kitten Bella, and I'd join in with all the rhymes. And then, when I learned to read by myself, I would read it out loud to Mum or Dad or Aunty Mags – or anyone else who was willing to listen. Crystal says I used to wear this silly red hat just like Sam in the book and whenever she read it to me I would always shout out the words, "I *am Sam! Sam I am!*" as if I was the most important person in the world.

I actually found my old copy of *Green Eggs and Ham* today, stuffed at the back of my bookshelf. I was sure I'd given it away years ago, to a school jumble sale or something, but there it was squashed between my Oxford dictionary and one of my Jacqueline Wilson books.

I took it down off the shelf and wiped away the dust. I'd read it so many times the pages were almost furry; all soft and curled up at the edges. Tucked inside the front cover was a photo. It was of me, Crystal *and* Bella – all sitting on my bed – reading *Green Eggs and Ham*.

I stared and stared at the photo. I'm wearing my little red hat just like Crystal said and I've got this look of total happiness on my face. Crystal's got her arm round me and she's laughing into the camera, her eyes sparkly and

bright. *Crystal by name and Crystal by nature,* Dad always used to say. She must've been about eight in the photo, but she already looks so grown-up for her age.

I rushed downstairs to show Mum. I don't know why but I just wanted her to see how happy we were. I burst into the living room shouting, "*I am Sam! Sam I am!*" like I was three again. Mum glanced up from her ironing and gave me a tight smile.

"Hey, look what I found," I said, holding the photo up to show her. "It's me in my silly red hat, remember?"

"What do you think you're doing, Sam?" She snatched the photo out of my hand and slapped it face down on the ironing board. "I thought you said you were sorting your things out for school. Term starts next week and I want you to be properly organized."

"I know, I was, but then I came across my old *Green Eggs and Ham* book and this photo

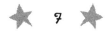

was stuck inside and it just got me thinking about Crystal and…" I trailed off.

Mum hates it when I talk about Crystal. She left home four months ago, the day after her eighteenth birthday, and ever since then I only have to mention her name and Mum goes off on one.

"This is all part of your problem," she grumbled, waving the iron about in the air. "I send you upstairs to do one simple job and two seconds later you've got caught up doing something completely different. That's what your teachers keep saying, isn't it? That you can't concentrate."

"No they don't." I picked up the photo and started backing out of the door. "Who actually said that anyway? Who said I can't concentrate?"

Mum set the iron down, sighing heavily. "Look, the point is, Sam, you're going into Year Eight and you're a clever girl. It's time to

knuckle down and show us what you're capable of, isn't it, Dave?" She looked over at my dad. He was sitting across the room with Bella on his lap, reading the paper and humming the same tune over and over. He's been funny since Crystal left as well. It's like he's there but not there. I could probably dance around the room wearing a black bin liner, with a bucket on my head, and he still wouldn't look up.

Mum strode over to him and pulled the paper down. "Dave! Are you even listening to me? I was just saying..."

I took the opportunity to slip out of the room. When Mum gets in a mood like that she could easily go on all night. We used to get on okay most of the time, but not any more.

Next morning at breakfast Mum picked straight up where she'd left off. I hadn't even poured my cereal before she started going on about

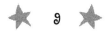

my grades and my homework and my A-tti-tude. That's her favourite word at the moment, "Attitude" – and according to Mum, mine's all wrong!

It's ever since Crystal left. Ever since she *turned down a place at one of the top universities in the country and moved in with her low-life boyfriend* – Mum's words by the way, not mine! Just because Crystal didn't want to follow the path Mum had carved out for her, Mum had decided to turn all her attention on me.

"I know you think I'm going on, Sam," she said, handing me a glass of juice, "but I just want you to make something of yourself, that's all. Anyway, I've got a big delivery at work, so I'm going up to get ready. As soon as you've eaten, I want you to finish sorting out your school stuff."

I sat there nibbling on a slice of toast. I don't know exactly what Mum thinks I'm going to do when I leave school. It's not like I'm going to be a brain surgeon or some sort of physics professor. The truth is, the only thing I've *ever* wanted to do is to be on the stage – but as far as Mum's concerned, acting is just a *hobby* and not something you do as a Proper Job. I was still sitting there thinking about my glittering future as a *Broadway Star* when there was a knock on the back door and Aunty Mags burst in.

"Hello, gorgeous," she said, throwing her bag down and giving me a big kiss. "Any chance of a cuppa?"

Aunty Mags is Dad's sister and we're really close. She only lives two streets away and she's always popping in to see me. I flicked the switch on the kettle and took down a mug. "My mum's in a mood," I said. "She wants me to be the next prime minister or something."

Aunty Mags smiled. "She's just worried about you, Sam. You know what she's like. Where's your dad?"

"He's already left for work. That's all he

does these days – work work work! Hey, you couldn't have a word with Mum, could you? Get her to ease up on me and tell her how serious I am about wanting to be an actress..." I clasped my hands together under my chin. "Please, Aunty Mags. For me. She's just in her room getting ready."

"Well, I'll try," she said slowly, popping a slice of bread in the toaster. "But she won't thank me for interfering."

I love my Aunty Mags so much. She's only a few years younger than Dad but she's always up for a laugh. Even when things go wrong she still manages to see the funny side. She poured another cup of tea for Mum, plonked everything on a tray and disappeared upstairs.

I waited for a few minutes and then followed her up. I didn't really expect it to do any good, but I was so sick of Mum nagging me all the time. I could just about hear Aunty Mags's voice through the door. She was telling Mum that it was time to give me a bit more freedom and let me make my own mistakes. That she couldn't live my life for me. I leaned in even closer, dying to hear what Mum would say to that – but just then my phone began to ring. It was my best friend, Ellie, back from her holiday in France.

"Come straight over!" she squealed down the phone. "I've got so much to tell you!"

"What? What's going on? Tell me now!"

"No, I can't! Just get over here!"

I popped my head round the door to ask Mum if I could go, and her and Aunty Mags both stopped talking in that really obvious way – like when you know you've interrupted some big secret.

"Can I go round to Ellie's?" I said. "She's just got back from holiday. I'll sort out my school stuff when I get back, promise."

Mum opened her mouth to say something and then closed it again. "Don't be too long," was all she managed. I backed out of the room before she could change her mind. The second the door closed behind me they started talking again and the last thing I heard as I trailed downstairs was Aunty Mags saying, "Of course Crystal's still upset, Rosy. What do you expect? I know you didn't mean it, but you can't expect Crystal to understand that..."

It was such a relief to get round to Ellie's. She'd been away for three weeks and I'd missed her like mad. She flung the door open and we threw our arms round each other as if we'd been separated for years.

"My holiday was a-*mazing*!" she cried. "It was boiling hot and the hotel had the best pool ever, and you'll never guess what... There was a disco and this boy asked me to dance and we ended up dancing all night and..." She stopped to breathe and then she hugged me again and whispered something in my ear, but I couldn't understand a word.

"What?" I said, laughing.

"He asked me out!" Her face turned crimson. "*And* the weirdest thing is he lives right near here. It's like the most unbelievable coincidence but he's practically my neighbour." The doorbell rang behind us and I jumped.

"Who's that? It's not him, is it?"

"Don't be daft. It's Phoebe and Polly," she said, ducking under my arm to let them in.

Phoebe and Polly came spilling through the door, laughing about something.

"Ellie's got a boyfriend!" I announced, before Ellie could tell them. "She met him on holiday and he asked her out at the hotel disco."

"*Sam!* He's not my *boyfriend* and don't start telling everyone!"

"No way," breathed Phoebe. "What's his name?"

"Eddie," said Ellie, blushing even more.

"And before you say anything, I know it sounds ridiculous, *Eddie and Ellie*, but you should see him. Honestly, I can't stop thinking about him."

"Well, I hope you're not going to forget all about *us* now you've got a boyfriend," I teased. "It's Friends First, remember?"

Ellie laughed, her eyes shining. "Of course I remember, silly. And for the hundredth time he is NOT my boyfriend!"

We grabbed some snacks from the kitchen and went upstairs. Polly told us all about staying with her mum in Spain and Phoebe had us in fits describing how awful it was sharing a tent with her little sister Sara on their camping holiday. And Ellie just went on and on about Eddie. I *was* pleased for her, but for some reason I always thought *I'd* be the first one to have a proper boyfriend. Not that Mum would ever let me. I could just imagine her face if I came home and said I had a date. She'd probably call the police and have him arrested!

"Did you all get a letter from Mandy about starting back at Star Makers?" I said, trying to change the subject just for a second. Star Makers is the drama club we go to on Saturday mornings. It's run by our drama teacher from school, Mandy, and it's totally brilliant.

"Mine was here waiting for me when we got back from the airport," said Ellie. "It had some weird poem in it."

"I reckon it's a clue about the new show. It must be a murder mystery or something," said Phoebe.

Ellie pulled a face. "I didn't understand a word. You know what I'm like, I don't even understand *normal* English half the time."

She picked up her letter, which was lying on top of a pile of clothes, and read the poem out to us.

The question of trust is one that you must
Be sure of — or you'll be in trouble!

So can you be sure
That the friend at the door
Isn't secretly somebody's double?

The clues don't make sense.
You're frightened and tense
A phantom — a warning — a light.
You try to get out,
You scream and you shout,
But who is that face in the night?

"I think it sounds really exciting," said Phoebe. "I've been trying to work out what it means all week."

"Maybe it's about a vampire," I said, jumping on top of Ellie and pinning her down on the bed. "Maybe the face in the night is a vampire come to suck your blood."

"Or *maybe* it's Eddie!" said Polly, jumping on top of me.

"Get off!" cried Ellie. "I can't breathe!"

"Yes, maybe it's Eddie," I said, "and he's after your blood! But don't worry, Ellie, we'll protect you."

"Get them off me, Phoebe," Ellie spluttered. But Phoebe jumped on too and knocked us all flying off the bed. We sat in a heap on the floor, laughing.

"I don't really care what show we do," said Polly. "I just can't wait to go back."

"Me neither," I agreed. "I know it's only been six weeks since we broke up but it feels more like six years."

I walked back home feeling so much happier. The new show would be brilliant whatever it was – and it was the perfect opportunity to show Mum, once and for all, how serious I was about acting.

2
The Phantom Face

I didn't have much time to worry about Mum over the next few days. School started back on Tuesday and from the second we arrived it was non-stop. There were new teachers to meet and a new timetable and a whole set of new rules and regulations now we were in Year Eight.

We stood about in the hallways, watching all the frightened Year Sevens scurrying around, trying to find their way from class to class, and it felt as if we'd been at Woodville Secondary for ever.

"Please don't tell me we were ever that small," said Polly.

"Hey, what do you mean?" groaned Phoebe.

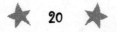

"I still *am* that small. I swear I didn't grow a single millimetre over the summer."

"Don't stand next to me then," I said. "I've grown loads in the last couple of months."

Ellie was rummaging through her bag, throwing things up in the air. "I can't find my timetable anywhere and I'm sure I'm supposed to be somewhere really important right this second."

"Have you seen *Eddie* since you got back?" I asked, retrieving her timetable from the pile of stuff she'd thrown on the floor. "We're all dying to meet him, you know."

"Well, I haven't seen him yet, but he has called me a few times."

"Are you sure he actually exists?" I teased. "He's not just one of your mad dreams, is he?"

"Shut up," said Ellie. "Of course he exists." She looked round at all of us. "I wasn't even going to tell you, but he's coming to meet me straight from drama on Saturday."

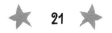

"No way!" squealed Phoebe and Polly, clutching hold of each other as if they'd never seen a boy before in their lives.

"But we usually go back to yours after drama," I said. "We've always done that. Can't you meet up with him on another day?"

Ellie stuffed the rest of her books and things back in her bag. "That was the only day he was free. He plays football on Sundays. Why don't you come over to mine on Sunday instead?"

"I'm busy on Sunday," I muttered, feeling a bit hurt. I wasn't about to arrange my weekend around Ellie and her new boyfriend.

"Hello, girls," said Mandy, rushing past. "All set for Saturday?"

"Can't wait!" said Phoebe.

"Hey, what's happened to your hair?" I called out. "It's *so* long!"

"Extensions," she called back. "It's my new look! What do you think?"

"Amazing," I said, and the others all nodded, agreeing.

She stopped suddenly, as if something had just occurred to her, and walked back to us. "Erm...Ellie, aren't you supposed to be showing the new Year Sevens where they have lunch right about now?"

"Oh no!" wailed Ellie. "I told you I was supposed to be somewhere important!" And she flew off down the corridor, tripping over the straps from her bag.

"It's nice to see some things never change," said Mandy, grinning. "See you on Saturday, girls."

I *love* the first day back at Star Makers – it's always so exciting to see everyone after the holidays. I'd arranged to meet Ellie outside, but she texted me to say she was running late so I went up without her. Most of the group were already there. Mandy was over at the piano with Phoebe's little sister Sara, and Phoebe and Polly were standing in the middle of the hall talking to two of the boys, Adam and Monty B. I dumped my bag on the front of the stage and went over to join them.

"Hey, Sam," said Polly. "Where's Ellie?"

"She's running late. Probably lost her shoes or something. What's going on? Why is your sister here, Phoebe?"

"It's a nightmare," groaned Phoebe. "I don't even want to talk about it. For some bizarre reason, Mandy has agreed to let Sara join Star Makers even though she won't be ten until the end of the year. Something to do with her being *grown up for her age,* which is like the biggest joke."

"She looks really cute," said Adam. "Kind of like a puppy."

"*Cute!*" spluttered Phoebe. "You won't be saying she's cute when you get to know her."

I looked across at Adam and then did a double-take and looked again. Something had changed. I mean, he's always been cute and I've always been like, *Hey, you're cute — big deal*, but suddenly my heart did a strange little flip and I could feel myself start to blush. Me, blush. I'm sorry but I. DO. NOT. BLUSH. I peered a bit closer. What was it? Was he taller? Was it because he was in Year Ten now? Was it...?

"Hi, Sam. How was your summer?" OMG, he was speaking to me. Staring straight into my eyes.

I smiled brightly. "Oh, you know, it was great. Non-stop fun and games!"

I looked away, blushing even more. *Non-stop fun and games?* What was I *talking* about? We all joke about fancying Adam, but this wasn't funny. Luckily, at that moment Mandy finished talking to Sara and called us over.

"Hello, you guys...welcome back and

welcome to Phoebe's sister, Sara, who's joined today." We all waved hi to Sara, who looked as if she was about to burst with excitement. "It's so fantastic to see you all, I've missed you like mad!" Mandy went on. "Now, we're actually going to start off this morning with a game called Murder Handshake."

"Oh, I *love* this game," I shouted out. "Can I be the detective, Mandy, *please*?"

"Yes, okay, Sam," said Mandy, laughing. "Go and wait outside while I choose the murderer."

We've played this game before in our drama lessons at school. One person is secretly chosen to be the murderer and then everyone walks round the hall shaking hands. When the murderer shakes your hand they tickle your palm and then you have to shake three more hands before you die.

A few minutes later Mandy called me back in and I walked around the hall trying to guess who the murderer was while the others began to fall to the floor.

"I'm too young to die!" shouted Monty B, the big joker of the group. He clutched hold of his chest, moaning and groaning as he sank to his knees.

"Do us all a favour and just die already," said Neesha, and then she dropped dead herself.

I was allowed three guesses but I got it first time. I could see straight away that Sara was the murderer. It was so obvious. She was grinning from ear to ear, and every time someone died she did a little hop and a skip.

We played a few more times and then Mandy called us over to sit in a circle.

"Sorry to start with such a gruesome game but our new show is all about a mysterious disappearance, a detective, and a lot of suspicious characters – so I thought it would be a good way to get us in the mood."

"Is that why you sent us that poem?" said Phoebe.

Mandy nodded. "You see, in the holidays I stayed in this really creepy castle in Scotland and there were all these rumours about it being haunted. I was so inspired, I decided to base our show on one of the rumours. It was about a missing girl called April and a mysterious butler who somehow managed to be in two places at once. I've called it *The Phantom Face*."

"I actually saw a real ghost once," said Monty B. "It was in my nan's attic and I swear it was staring right at me."

"Oh my God, yeah," said Neesha. "It probably took one look at you and dropped dead with fright."

"Erm, it was a *ghost*, Neesha, so I expect it was dead already."

Just then Ellie came bursting through the doors. I could see straight away why she was late; she'd obviously spent ages getting ready for Eddie. She was wearing a new top and loads of make-up and she'd done something different with her hair.

"Sorry, sorry," she said, out of breath and flustered. She squashed in next to me and gave me a hug. "Have I missed anything?"

"Not really. Mandy's just about to tell us about the new show – it's called *The Phantom Face*. Monty B saw a ghost but he scared it half to death. And Phoebe's sister Sara's joined."

"Hello, Ellie," said Mandy. "Lovely top!"

"Thanks, Mandy. Sorry I'm late. Have you explained about that weird poem yet?"

"That weird poem, as you put it, is actually the opening number and I was just about to play it for you." She got up to go across to the piano.

"Oh, can't you talk about the characters a bit first?" I said. "I really, *really* want a main part this time, Mandy."

"You always really *really* want a main part," said Monty B.

I was just about to tell him to take a flying leap but Mandy gave me a look and carried on.

"Well, basically it's about this big family who are staying in an ancient castle for a wedding. Two of the guests, Laura and her older brother Ben, keep noticing a face at the window and it turns out to be a girl called April who disappeared four years earlier. Laura and Ben decide to try and solve the mystery of the missing girl themselves, but the more questions they ask, the more trouble they find themselves in."

"It sounds quite serious," said Tara, peering at Mandy through her little round glasses.

"I suppose it is in a way, but there are some funny characters as well, like Mr. Biscuit the detective. He doesn't have a clue about how to do his buttons up straight, let alone how to solve a crime. Anyway, I had great fun writing it, so I hope you'll have fun performing it."

We spent the rest of the session playing games and talking about *The Phantom Face*. Mandy got us into groups and we had to make freeze-frames of different scenes from the show. First off, we did a group of people arriving at the castle for the wedding, and then a detective arresting someone while everyone else looks on horrified. We also got into pairs to try out the scene where the two children see the face at the window for the first time.

It was brilliant to be back with everyone, messing about and having a laugh, but for some annoying reason I couldn't stop peeking over at Adam – like *every two seconds!* He just looked *so* cute. I tried not to make it obvious, but it was like my eyes were attached to magnets or something.

When it was time to leave, I told Mandy I really, *really* wanted to be Laura, and she said she'd give out the scripts next week and that the auditions would be in a few weeks' time. I tried to find Ellie to ask her who she wanted to be, but she'd disappeared into the loos to redo her make-up for about the tenth time. I could tell she was nervous about meeting Eddie, even though she kept saying he was just a friend, not a boyfriend. I waited for her to come out and we went downstairs together.

Eddie was waiting in the car park. He was wearing blue Converse All Stars, and a bright blue baseball cap pulled right down over his eyes. I suppose he was quite cute in a geeky sort of way, but nothing like as gorgeous as Adam.

"We're going into town if you want to come, Sam," said Ellie. "I'd really like you to." But I shook my head. I didn't want to tag along when it was obvious they wanted to be by themselves.

I tried to call Crystal on the way home, but it went straight to voicemail. She hadn't been in touch for ages and I really wanted to tell her what was going on. We've always been close, even though she's six years older than me, and I hated not knowing exactly what she was up to.

When I was little we used to spend loads of time together. She'd look after me while Mum was at work. She'd do my hair and let me try on her clothes and make-up. The best was when Mum and Dad went out in the evening. As soon as they left she'd make us hot chocolate with loads of froth on top, and then let me stay up and watch DVDs till I fell asleep curled up next to her on the couch. She just had this way of making everything seem exciting, even if it was just watching old Disney movies.

She was brilliant at keeping in touch when she first left. She rang me every week, full of news – moving in with Tyler, going to gigs, making lots of jewellery to sell. But these last few weeks, I hadn't heard a word. I sat at the bus stop, staring at my phone. I didn't even know where she was living, not her actual address – she could be anywhere. It was beginning to feel like she'd disappeared into thin air.

News at Last...

I kept on calling Crystal all weekend but she still didn't answer her phone or call me back. It was awful. I was so used to talking to her whenever I wanted and now weeks had passed without a word. She could be ill or in trouble or anything. I thought about what I'd heard Aunty Mags say that day in Mum's bedroom:

Of course Crystal's still upset, Rosy. What do you expect?

I've never really understood what happened between Mum and Crystal. They used to row all the time about boyfriends and make-up and curfews – normal stuff – but then, on the night of Crystal's eighteenth birthday, they had this massive fight – **THE FIGHT TO END ALL FIGHTS** – and the next day Crystal was gone.

I wanted her to come home so much. I know lots of people move out by the time they're eighteen – but not after a massive fight like that. If only I could find out what Mum said to Crystal that night. I had tried asking her but she always managed to come up with some excuse, like it was too difficult to explain or I was too young to understand. If I could just find out what it was, then maybe I'd be able to talk to Crystal about it and put things right – if I ever heard from her again!

I was dying to discuss it with Ellie on Monday – ask her what she thought I should do – but she was so excited about her *date* with Eddie that I couldn't get a word in edgeways. It was like we'd swapped places or something. Usually it's me going on about my weekend on a Monday morning, hogging all the limelight, but Polly and Phoebe were hanging on to Ellie's every word, giggling and carrying on as if they'd never heard of someone going out with a boy before.

"Ellie and Eddie," sighed Phoebe. "It sounds so romantic. I wonder who *my* first boyfriend will be?"

"Your first and *only* boyfriend will probably be Monty B, won't it?" I snapped.

Phoebe swung her bag at me. "Shut up, no it won't," she cried, turning crimson. "What about you and Adam then?"

"What *about* me and Adam?" I said, cool as anything, but I could feel my face start to burn up too and I rushed on ahead before I gave myself away. I'd been thinking about Adam non-stop since drama, whenever I wasn't worrying about Crystal. It was like he'd got stuck inside my head, and it was driving me nuts.

On Friday night, Aunty Mags came over for dinner. Mum was still at work so she got busy, bustling about the kitchen, making a big pot of chilli con carne. Mum runs her own florist shop called *Everything's Rosy*. She's become quite well known in the local area, doing the flowers for big weddings and other special occasions, but it means she's off really early in the morning and often doesn't get in until late.

"You haven't told me what my mum said when you had your little chat the other week," I said to Aunty Mags, stirring the chilli so it didn't stick to the bottom of the pan. "And what was she saying about Crystal? I heard you say something to her about Crystal being upset. I haven't heard from her in ages, you know. I'm really worried."

"Listen, Sam, I know it's difficult for you. I want your mum and Crystal to make up as much as you, but it's going to take some time."

"But why do you think Crystal hasn't been in touch? And what did they row about anyway?

She used to call me at least once a week, even if it was just to say hi."

Aunty Mags put her arm round me and gave me a hug. "I really don't know, lovey, but Crystal's eighteen and she's living her own life now. When I was eighteen I went off travelling round the world and I was *terrible* at keeping in touch. She'll call you soon, I'm sure of it. Come on, you old worry guts, let's have a boogie!"

I wasn't so sure that Crystal *would* call me, and I still didn't know what was going on, but Aunty Mags just has this magical way of making everything seem a bit brighter. She put on an old eighties CD and we danced round the kitchen, singing at the tops of our voices, while the chilli bubbled away on the stove and we waited for Mum and Dad to come home.

I couldn't wait to get to drama that Saturday. Mandy was bringing the scripts for *The Phantom*

Face and we were going to have a proper read-through.

"Please, please, *please* can I read Laura's part?" I said as soon as I walked into the hall. "I did tell you I wanted to be Laura, didn't I?"

"Erm, only about six hundred times," said Mandy, laughing. "But we're going to do things a bit differently for this production – I'll explain in a sec."

When everyone had a script, Mandy asked us to get into three groups.

"I want all the people who think they'd like to try out for Laura over there, all the people who like the sound of Ben's part, down here, and if you fancy trying out for one of the funny characters, sit in front of me."

There was a load of noise and excitement as everyone got up and moved into one of the three groups.

"Oh, I don't know who I want to be, Mandy," wailed Ellie. "I don't even understand the story

★ 40 ★

yet. I know there's a face and someone called Biscuit, but that's about it."

"Come into the funny group, Ellie. Just try not to lose your script this morning because I won't find that amusing at all!"

Once we'd sorted ourselves out, Mandy gave each group a small passage to learn from different parts of the script.

"I'd like you to get a really good feel for the characters and then we'll watch your scenes in about half an hour. But I'm not going to decide any of the parts today."

I was in a group with Catharine, Polly, Sara and Tara.

"I'd never be brave enough to try out for a big part normally," said Tara, pushing her glasses up her nose. "I only came into this group because Laura sounds like a timid sort of character and I thought I might be quite good at that – if I'm even brave enough to audition!"

"I never get scared at auditions," I said. "I can't wait to get up there and show Mandy what I can do!"

"I never get scared either," said Sara. "Phoebe's the one who won't say boo to a goose! You should see her sometimes – it's hilarious."

"What's she saying?" Phoebe called out from across the hall. "Put a gag on her, can't you, Sam?"

"It's okay," said Catharine. "I'll make sure she behaves." Catharine's in Year Nine, so she's about a year older than the rest of us. She had the main part in our first show and she's brilliant at singing *and* acting. I was gutted she was even *thinking* about being Laura.

"I don't really mind who I am," she said suddenly, as if she could read my mind. "I only came into this group because I'm rubbish at being funny."

"Same," said Polly. "I had the main part

last term, so I'm not expecting it this time anyway."

"That just leaves me then," I said, practically rubbing my hands together. "Can I go first?" I called out to Mandy.

"Hang on, Sam. Have you even read it through yet?"

She was over with the group of boys who wanted to try out for Ben. There was Adam and a couple of the others – Sandeep and Jason.

Our group had to learn the passage where Laura tells Ben about the face at the window for the first time. We spent ages memorizing it, testing each other over and over before it was time to act it out. Laura had to sound scared but excited as well. The face at the window frightens her but she can't wait to tell Ben all about it. I tried to get the balance just right: spooked by the face, but thrilled at the prospect of solving a mystery with my big brother.

"That was fantastic, Sam," said Mandy,

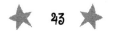

when I'd had my turn at performing. "Now after break, when everyone's had a go, I'd like each of the Lauras to pair up with one of the Bens and we'll put the scenes together. That's what I meant about doing things differently this time."

I looked across at the group of Bens. There was no way I wanted to be with Adam. In the first Star Maker's show, my character was actually married to his character so we did practically all our scenes together, but that was before I started blushing every time he even looked in my general direction!

As soon as Mandy said it was time for break, I rushed straight over to Sandeep and asked him to be my partner, willing him to say yes.

"What do you mean?" cried Adam, pretending to sound all offended. "We're married, in case you'd forgotten, and I don't want you going off with anyone else, especially not Sandeep."

My face started to burn up and I dashed back over to the other side of the room before I said something completely moronic. There was no way I could get up on a stage and act with Adam – not if he kept saying things like that – it would be a total disaster!

"Me and Sandeep are partners," I announced to Mandy straight after break, just to make sure she didn't put me with anyone else. I hung onto Sandeep's arm and practically forced him to stand glued to my side while Mandy sorted out the pairs. I really wanted a big part and I wasn't about to let some stupid boy ruin my chances, however cute he was.

In the end Adam went with Catharine, Jason paired up with Polly, and Tara decided she didn't want such a big part after all. There was no one left for Sara so Adam said he'd do the scene twice, once with Catharine and once with Sara.

"I honestly do think *I* should be Laura," said

Sara. "I'm the youngest for a start and I'm so good at acting, aren't I, Phoebe?"

"So good at showing off you mean!" said Phoebe.

"Yeah, you sound just like Sam," said Monty B. "You're not related by any chance, are you?"

I glared at Monty B. "I am not a show-off!" I said. "I'm just sure of myself. There is a difference you know."

The scene went really well. Sandeep was brilliant and I was positive Mandy would cast him as Ben when she came to choose the parts. I suppose some of the others were good as well, but we were easily the best pair. When we'd all had our turn, Mandy collected the scripts and we finished with a few games.

We were just about to leave when Arthur turned up. He's the man who rents Mandy the hall and we all think he's a bit bonkers – including Mandy. In the first term he accidentally sold all our costumes at the annual church jumble sale, and last term he misprinted the programmes for our show so that they said *Trash* instead of *Crash*. He acts in a group himself, called *The Players*, and he's always popping in to see what we're doing. Mandy says it's because he really loves acting, but personally I think it's because he secretly loves *her*.

"Oh, hello there, Mandy. I do hope all is forgiven," he said, slinking into the room as if he half expected to be pelted with eggs or something. "Let bygones be bygones – that's what I always say."

"Is it now?" said Mandy through gritted teeth. She wasn't going to forget about the programme fiasco that easily. "How about bye-*byes*, Arthur, rather than byg*ones*?"

"Oh yes! Haha! Very funny. Bye-*byes*," he spluttered, a load of biscuit crumbs spraying out from his beard. "Bye-*byes* rather than by*gones*. Oh yes! I get it! Ahem. Well I can see you're busy. So glad we've been able to put the little matter of the programmes behind us and resume our special friendship. Marvellous."

"Bye-*bye*," said Mandy as Arthur spun round and swept out of the room.

I looked around for Ellie, expecting her to be collapsed on the floor laughing, but she was too busy looking into a little mirror and putting on her lipgloss.

"Eddie's meeting me again today," she said as we were walking down the stairs at the end of the session. "Are you sure you won't come with us this time? I really want you to get to know him. We can all be friends together, you know."

"Sorry, Ellie, I've got plans," I said airily. "You wouldn't believe how busy my Saturday afternoons are these days."

I trailed to the bus stop, thinking about Ellie

and Eddie. It was so weird to see her going out with someone – like she'd been doing it all her life. I might be confident about acting but when it came to boys I didn't seem to have the first clue. I was dying for Adam to fancy me, but if he actually asked me out I'd probably run a mile in the opposite direction.

I got off the bus and walked home as slowly as I could. I knew the house would be empty. No loud music. No Crystal gabbing away to all her friends and making a huge mess. Everyone's always saying I'm the biggest loudmouth – desperate to be centre of attention – but I had to be loud just to compete with Crystal.

I let myself in and listened for a second, but there wasn't a sound. Of course there wasn't. Crystal was gone and the sooner I got used to it the better.

I was just about to go upstairs when I noticed there was a letter for me lying on the mat by the door. It was quite big and it looked kind of official, like the sort of letters they send from school or from the bank.

I sat down on the bottom of the stairs and tore along the top of the envelope. There was a beautiful card inside. It was an invitation, printed on that special sort of paper that people make themselves. The kind that's so fragile it feels as if it might crumble in your hands. The words were small and delicate and there were twirls and swirls all the way around the edges.

My heart started to race. I couldn't believe it. I hugged the card to my chest, shaking.

It was an invitation to a wedding.

Crystal's wedding.

So Many Secrets

No way *no way* NO WAY. Crystal getting married? It was crazy. I couldn't believe it. Not Crystal. Crystal was wild. Crystal did whatever she wanted. Getting married was what grown-ups did and Crystal had always turned her nose up at anything to do with growing up. **LIFE IS FOR LIVING,** she used to shout at Mum – and she was out living hers practically every night of the week. At parties and concerts, hanging out with her mates. And now Crystal was getting *married*?

I held the invitation out in front of me and read it again.

"To the world you may be one person…
but to one person you may be the world."

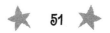

Crystal and Tyler
invite you to share in their love and happiness...
At: St. Michael's Church, 12.30 p.m.
Reception and lunch: Fable Manor Town Hall,
1.30 p.m.
On: Saturday 28th November

I'd only met Tyler a few times before Crystal moved out. He was quite a bit older than her usual boyfriends and Mum was so against the whole relationship that he hardly ever came round. He wrote music and played in a band called The Garlic Pickers. Crystal used to go along to all their gigs, desperate for him to notice her. And of course he did. *Everyone* noticed Crystal. But *getting married?*

I was still sitting there in a state of total shock when I heard Mum's car pull up in the drive. I tried to slip the invitation back into the envelope but there was something else in there. It was a small note scribbled in Crystal's tiny handwriting.

Sorry Sam, I know I should've called but it's been mad! And anyway, I wanted to surprise you. Can you believe it?!!! I'll come and meet you from school one day next week. Oh, and don't breathe a word to anyone — especially not Mum and Dad.

Luv u loads xxxxxxxxxx

She was right about surprising me. I would've been less surprised if she'd said she was joining the army!

I carried the invitation around with me all week. I didn't dare leave it anywhere, in case Mum or Dad got their hands on it. I really wanted to tell them – it felt like such a big secret to keep – but I had to keep my mouth shut, at least until I'd spoken to Crystal myself. It was a nightmare pretending everything was normal, but at least I knew she was okay.

Ellie noticed that something was up straight

away. "Is anyone there?" she said first thing on Monday, waving her hand in front of my face. "I've just spent the last ten minutes telling you about how Eddie and Adam go to the same school and you haven't been listening to a word. What's wrong?"

"I know what's wrong," said Polly, teasing. "She's working out how to convince Mandy to give her the biggest part in the show, right, Sam?"

I did want a big part in the show but that was the last thing on my mind right that second. I was dying to tell Ellie about the wedding – I've always told her everything – but I wasn't allowed. I wasn't allowed to tell Ellie, or Mum and Dad, or Aunty Mags, or *anyone*. How on earth was I supposed to keep something *this* BIG a secret?

I kept expecting Crystal to turn up at school. I rushed out every day, but the week passed and she didn't show. By the time Saturday came round, I was beginning to wonder if I'd dreamed the whole thing or if the invitation was just a wind-up. Until I actually heard Crystal say the words herself, it just wouldn't seem real. And then, just when I thought things couldn't get any more stressful, Mum dropped THE SECOND BOMBSHELL OF THE WEEK.

We were having breakfast on Saturday morning and she started going on about school. It was the usual thing: *"You're not working hard enough...blah...your grades are slipping... blah...your A-tti-tude is all wrong...blah blah..."*

I was sitting there totally switched off – deep in my own thoughts about Crystal's wedding and how Mum and Dad were going to flip when they found out – when she suddenly mentioned something about Saturday mornings. My head snapped up.

"What did you say?"

Mum sighed and rolled her eyes. "What is it about my family? Why don't any of you listen to me? I was just saying that I've found this fantastic tutor, Mrs. Raja, but she's only available on Saturday mornings."

"Never mind," I said. "It's not like you'd expect me to give up drama to have extra maths lessons or something."

Mum coughed and looked down at her coffee. There was a long silence.

"Hang on a minute. You have got to be joking. I am not giving up Star Makers – not for anything and certainly not for some stupid *tutor!*"

"Calm down, Sam. For goodness' sake! I know you love acting, but at the end of the day it's just a *hobby*. I've been telling you for weeks that you've got to start taking your schoolwork more seriously."

"I *am* taking it seriously! What else do you want me to do? I'm in the top set for nearly all my subjects and I'm not behind with any of my coursework. This isn't about me at all, is it?

Just because Crystal didn't go to uni, you've decided to ruin *my* life instead." I leaped up and ran towards the door. "Stop trying to control me!" I yelled. "You can't arrange my life like you arrange one of your bouquets at the shop. I'm a *person*, Mum! Not a flower!"

I stormed out of the room and upstairs.

"Oh, stop being so dramatic, Sam," Mum called after me. "I know you're not a flower!"

She followed me up and sat on the edge of my bed, twisting my covers round and round her finger. "Look, Sam, I don't want to fight with you all the time. I had enough of that with your sister. I haven't even made any arrangements for the tutor to come – it was just something I was discussing with Dad. And I'm not going to stop you going to Star Makers, not this term, but...look...I really don't want you taking on too much there..."

"But *Mum*!"

"I mean it, Sam. You need to focus on your

schoolwork and you know what will happen if you take on a main role. You'll have loads of lines to learn and your homework will slip and you'll be too distracted to concentrate at school. I know it seems harsh, but it is for your own good."

"But I've told Mandy I want to be Laura and it *is* the biggest part. I have to take on the big roles if I'm going to be a proper actress. That's all I care about. You know I've always wanted to be on the stage."

Mum sighed, biting the inside of her cheek. "I know, Sam, and I do understand, but your education is so much more important. I had to give up my place at university and I've *always* regretted it. And look at your sister. You do realize she could have been at university *right now*, making something of herself. But she's given it all up to sell...*jewellery*."

She spat out the word "jewellery" as if she'd just eaten a mouthful of maggots. Crystal makes

★ 58 ★

the most beautiful crystal jewellery – delicate silver necklaces and bracelets decorated with different coloured sparkly stones. She designs them all herself with these funky patterns and really unusual shapes, but as far as Mum's concerned it's just not a "proper" career.

I gave up arguing after that. There was nothing I could say or do which would make her realize how serious I was about being an actress – but I wasn't about to give up on my dreams just because Crystal had left home and turned everything upside down.

As soon as I got to drama later that morning, I started to feel better. Everyone was already in a circle and Mandy was busy handing round the scripts. I glanced across at Adam. He was sitting with Catharine and they were laughing about something. We used to muck about and have a laugh all the time last term – but I can't imagine even *talking* to him now without saying something completely stupid.

"Come and sit over here," Ellie called out to me. "I saved a space for you."

Mandy handed me a script and I sat down by Ellie. I didn't want to think about Crystal's wedding or Mum and all her stupid rules – I just wanted to get on with the auditions.

"Have a good look through," Mandy was saying, "and then we'll get into groups and act out some of the scenes. If you're trying out for Laura or Ben, stay in the pairs you were in last week but join up with some other people to do your scenes. It's not really an audition, but I do need to take one more look at the Laura and Ben couples."

"What are you doing later?" I asked Ellie. "My mum's doing my head in and it would be great if I could hang out at yours for a bit."

"Oh, I'm sorry, Sam. I'm meeting Eddie again after drama." She blushed a bit. "But I really wish you'd come with us this time. What's up with your mum, anyway?"

"She thinks I'm about to fail every subject at school and she's found some Saturday morning tutor for me. It's a total nightmare."

"I had to have a tutor in Year Six. It's not that bad."

"Yes but, Ellie...*Saturday mornings!*" I said, not sure Ellie was getting how serious this was.

"Any idea who you'd like to try out for, Ellie?" said Mandy, coming over.

Ellie shook her head. "I still don't know, to tell you the truth."

"I'm trying out for Laura," I said. "Did I tell you, Mandy? I really want a big part this time. I know I'd be brilliant."

Mandy laughed. "You're very confident, Sam. Choose a scene then, and I'll come round and have a listen in a sec."

I smiled and nodded but inside I didn't feel quite as confident as usual. Ellie was dropping me for Eddie, Mum thought having some stupid

tutor was more important than Star Makers, Crystal was *supposedly* getting married – and I couldn't seem to get Adam out of my head. Everything around me was changing and I didn't like it one little bit.

We ended up doing the scene where the detective comes to the castle to question Laura and Ben about the face at the window. Monty B joined me and Sandeep to be Mr. Biscuit, and Ellie was his trusted assistant, Sugar.

"Don't you think it would be funnier if we added some more biscuit jokes?" said Monty B when we'd read it through once.

"You don't mean you're going to change it, do you?" I said.

"No, not change it exactly, just embellish it a bit."

"Stop using clever words," complained Ellie. "What does 'embellish' mean anyway?"

Monty B grinned. "It means to adorn or add interest to the piece," he said.

"*What?*" said Ellie, even more confused.

"I think he means he's going to add bits just to annoy Mandy," said Sandeep.

And Monty did add bits and Mandy did get annoyed, but it was really funny. Ellie got the worst fit of giggles, and the more she laughed, the more biscuit jokes he made. He ended the scene by saying, "The trouble with this case is there's not one single *crumb* of evidence," and Ellie literally had to be helped off the stage, she was so hysterical.

"Okay, I'm changing the detective's name," said Mandy. "What on earth was I thinking? And you can forget all about having that part, Monty B."

"Don't say that, Mandy," said Monty B. "I'd make a great digestive...er...I mean detective, wouldn't I, Ellie?"

But Ellie was laughing too hard to answer.

It was fun watching the others perform. Catharine was just as good as usual, but I think

Sara was the biggest surprise. She didn't get all the lines right and she looked a bit young to be Laura – but she was *so* loud and confident. I wasn't that worried about either of them getting the part to be honest, but I did make sure to tell Mandy one last time that I really wanted to be Laura – just in case she'd forgotten.

When we left to go home, Eddie was waiting for Ellie at the bottom of the stairs. That was three weeks in a row! We said hello and Ellie asked me to come with them again, but I thought Eddie gave me a funny look, like he didn't want me to, so I made up an excuse. He was looking much more confident these days and I couldn't help feeling that same twinge of jealousy that he was there, taking my best friend away from me, just when I needed her most.

5

Head-Over-Heels

The week flew by and somehow I managed to push Crystal's invitation to the back of my mind. She didn't turn up at school or call me, but I figured she was probably just busy with arrangements for the wedding. Mum's done the flowers for loads of big weddings and she says the bride always ends up totally stressed out.

There wasn't really time to worry about it anyway. We had tons more homework now we were in Year Eight and every single teacher seemed to think their subject was the most important. Last year I was in trouble all the time for messing around in class, but I knew I had to keep my grades as high as possible in *every* subject if I was going to convince Mum not to book that tutor. Ellie still wanted to have a giggle and muck about, but I just couldn't afford to pass notes back and forth about how dreamy Eddie was or what she should wear on Saturday. She'd sent me a note that morning during French – something about meeting up with Eddie after drama – but I'd stuffed it in my bag without answering. It was Friday and I'd been trying to get all my homework down in my diary before the bell rang.

"Why are you being such a boring old stick-in-the-mud?" she complained at the end of the day. We were in the cloakroom getting our stuff and she'd been having a go at me for the past ten minutes. "Eddie says it's because you're jealous I've got all the attention for once – but I told him that was rubbish."

"It is rubbish," I said. "How comes he's such an expert all of a sudden? He doesn't even know me. And why were you talking about me behind my back?"

Ellie blushed a bit. "It wasn't behind your back, Sam. Okay, I *was* talking about you, but only because I want Eddie to get to know you. Why won't you just come out with us one Saturday? It's not like I haven't asked you about a hundred million times."

"Fine, I will! Just to stop you going on about it. But not this week. Let's go back to yours after drama tomorrow for a change. Girls only! We haven't done that for ages. We're getting our parts, so we could start practising and Phoebe and Polly could come as well. You don't want to be one of those girls who drops all her friends the second you get a *boyfriend,* do you?"

"He is *not* my boyfriend!" said Ellie, getting very wound up. "When are you going to realize?"

"When you stop seeing him *every* Saturday," I muttered. "So can we go over to yours tomorrow or not?"

"Hey, do you mind if we practise at mine instead?" said Phoebe, as she came in to grab her coat. "My mum's going out for the day and I've got to look after Sara."

Ellie shrugged. "Okay then. We'll go to Phoebe's tomorrow after drama, but the following Saturday you have to promise you'll come out with me and Eddie."

I promised with my fingers crossed behind my back. I didn't want to go out with boring old Eddie – Ellie was welcome to him as far as I was concerned. I wanted to go out with *Adam,* but it's not like that was ever going to happen.

Aunty Mags was waiting for me when I came out of school, standing across the road by her car. I thought something might be wrong for a second, but she was grinning like mad and waving a newspaper at me.

"Hurry up, Sam," she called out. "I really need your help with something."

I crossed over to meet her. "What's going on?"

"Look at this," she said. "I was leafing through the local paper at work this morning and there are some chocolate-brown Labrador puppies for sale right near here!"

"And?" I looked at her, confused.

"And I've always wanted one of course! So anyway," she went on, practically pushing me into the car. "I called the woman, her name is Mrs. Dale, and she said we could come and have a look today."

"Do you mean you want me to help you choose?"

She ran round to the other side of the car. "Yes! I want you to help me choose," she said, climbing in. "Isn't it so, so exciting!"

We drove along, chatting about school. Aunty Mags wanted to know all about my new Year Eight teachers; who I liked best and what we were doing in each subject. I thought about asking her a few questions of my own – like what my mum actually said to Crystal on the night of her eighteenth birthday party – but I was having such a nice time I didn't want to spoil the mood.

"Now be strict with me, Sam," said Aunty Mags as we drew up outside the house. "I'm only buying *one*, however cute they are."

Mrs. Dale opened the door with one of the puppies clasped to her chest. It was the most adorable thing I'd ever seen in my life! It had the softest brown fur and was easily small enough to fit into the palm of my hand. I thought Mrs. Dale looked quite familiar for a second, but I wasn't sure where I'd seen her before.

"Come in, come in," she said, leading us into the living room. "It's a complete tip, I'm afraid, but find yourselves somewhere to sit down and you can meet the pups. This is their mum, Carla." She patted a big, chocolate-brown Labrador. "She's feeling very proud of herself and very protective, but she won't mind you having a cuddle."

The rest of the puppies were squashed into an old dog basket filled with blankets and quilts. Carla lay down by the basket and three of the puppies hopped out, clambering over each other to snuggle into her and feed.

"How on earth are we going to choose?" cried Aunty Mags. Her eyes were bright with excitement and I half-wished I was getting one of the puppies myself. Not that Bella would be very impressed! She already thinks she's Queen of the Household, so I don't expect she'd take too kindly to a puppy.

"Here, have a cuddle," said Mrs. Dale, holding out the little ball of fur in her arms. "This one here's the runt of the litter. That's why I'm carrying him around. He keeps getting squashed in the basket and pushed out of the way." I reached out for the tiny puppy and he snuggled into me, trying to climb right into my coat. "This is the one, Aunty Mags," I said. "He might be the smallest but just look at his eyes and little paws and his tiny tongue and..." Just then the front door slammed.

"Oh, that'll be my youngest home from school. Come in and say hello," she called out. "Some people are here choosing a puppy. I'll just go and put on the kettle," she said to us.

Mrs. Dale's son came straight into the living room to see who was about to steal away one of his precious puppies. I looked up to say hello but my mouth dropped open.

It was Adam.

Mrs. – Dale's – son – was – Adam.

"Oh hi, Sam," he said, as if it was completely normal to come home from school and find me sitting in his living room cuddling one of his puppies.

"W-what are you doing here?" I stammered.

"Erm, I'm not sure... Oh yes, I know, I live here."

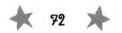

"You live here? With Mrs. Dale?"

"Well, she is my mum," he laughed.

I could feel myself start to burn up. I sounded like a complete idiot. No wonder I thought I recognized Mrs. Dale when she opened the door.

"This little one's called Riley," said Adam, squashing down between us on the couch.

"Hello, Adam," said Aunty Mags. "That's funny – you two knowing each other. Have you got a favourite?"

"It's the one Sam's holding actually, although I don't think her cat would be too happy about it."

"Oh no, it's not for me," I said. "It's for Aunty Mags. I've just come along to help her choose – not that I know much about dogs. I know loads about cats though. My cat's a Persian Blue. She's called Bella. That actually means 'beautiful' you know, in Italian. She's really old now – she just sleeps all the time – but she used to win first prize in *all* the cat shows..." I trailed off, feeling more stupid than ever.

Adam lifted Riley off my lap and carried him over to Carla. As soon as he put him down, the poor little pup nuzzled into her and started to feed. "He needs as much milk as he can get, but the others keep pushing him around and he doesn't get a look-in!"

Just then two of the other feeding puppies nudged Riley firmly out of the way. He sat back, looking dazed, and we all burst out laughing.

"I'm totally smitten, I'm afraid," said Aunty Mags.

Mrs. Dale came back in from the kitchen with some mugs of tea and a plate of biscuits. "This is Sam from drama, Mum," said Adam. "Didn't you recognize her?"

"Well the last time you saw me I was a deadly virus and I was wearing a black and green mask, so it's not very likely," I said.

"Oh, you were fantastic," laughed Mrs. Dale.

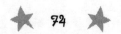

"I remember. But you look much prettier with your mask off."

I blushed all over again and leaned over the puppies to hide my face. I'd *need* a mask at this rate, if I was going to turn brilliant red every time I was anywhere near Adam.

Mrs. Dale explained to Aunty Mags that the puppies wouldn't be ready to leave Carla for another week or so. We had a few more cuddles with Riley and a couple of biscuits, and then we set off home.

"See you tomorrow," said Adam. "I think we're going to find out our parts, aren't we?"

I nodded, mumbled something completely moronic, and dragged Aunty Mags out to the car. I couldn't believe I'd just spent the afternoon over at Adam's house – it was crazy, and *so* embarrassing. I'd babbled on like a total twit. I really needed to talk to Ellie – and fast.

"I think someone's got a little crush," Aunty Mags teased when we were on our way.

"I have not got a crush," I said firmly. But my face started to burn up AGAIN. What on earth was happening to me? Maybe I did have a crush – and not such a *little* one either – but I wasn't about to tell Aunty Mags.

I had an even bigger surprise when I got in. Mum and Dad were both home from work and they were drinking champagne. For a crazy second I wondered if they were celebrating Crystal's news; that she'd actually been in touch and told them about the wedding.

"What's going on?" I said.

"I've had a really exciting day at work!" Mum grinned, practically bubbling over with excitement. She took a sip of champagne. "Remember I told you about Sophia Malone getting married...well this woman called Lavender rang – she's the wedding planner – and she's only chosen *Everything's Rosy* to do the flowers!"

"You're kidding, Mum, that's amazing!

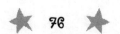

Sophia Malone! I saw her in that TV drama just a few weeks ago and she was brilliant."

"I'm so proud of you, Rosy," said Dad, beaming. "Just imagine – *Everything's Rosy* doing the flowers for someone so well known. You'll get tons of publicity."

"I know," said Mum. "It's like a dream come true."

Mum had built up *Everything's Rosy* from nothing, all by herself. She'd worked all hours of the day and night, from when it was just a tiny florist on a little alley off the high street to the huge success it was today.

"Well done, Mum. There's no stopping you now!" I was really proud of her too.

"Everything's rosy for Rosy!" joked Dad and he began to sing some song from years ago, dancing Mum round the room.

"When is the wedding?" I said as they twirled around me. "It's not on Christmas Day or something daft like that, is it?"

"No, it's before Christmas." Mum pulled away from Dad and fished her diary out of her bag. "It's at the end of November," she said, leafing through the pages. I fixed my eyes on the diary, desperately trying to remember the date of Crystal's wedding. It was definitely in November but I couldn't remember the exact date. What was it? What *was* it?

"Here it is," said Mum. "Saturday the 28th of November."

6
Poor old Sandeep!

I raced upstairs and pulled out Crystal's invitation. I kept on staring at it as if somehow by magic the date would change. But no, it was still there, as clear as anything. Crystal and Tyler were getting married on Saturday the 28th of November. I grabbed my phone to call Crystal. My hands were actually trembling and it was difficult to press the numbers properly. I managed it eventually but there was a loud click and it went straight to voicemail. *"Call me,"* I hissed. *"I need to talk to you. It's urgent – like* really *urgent!"*

I kept checking my phone every five seconds but she didn't call back. How was I supposed to keep quiet now? I *had* to tell Mum. They might be in the middle of some massive row and she might think Tyler was a total waste of space but there's no way she'd want to miss Crystal's actual wedding.

Mum was making breakfast when I came down in the morning.

"Pinch me to make sure I'm not dreaming," she said, laughing. "I hardly slept a wink."

"You're not dreaming," I said. And even if she was, it was all about to turn into one massive nightmare. Sophia Malone and Crystal were both getting married in eight weeks' time on exactly the same day.

"I've got a little surprise of my own," Dad announced suddenly. He took an envelope out of his pocket and waved it about in front of Mum's face.

"What's that?" she asked suspiciously. "You know I don't like surprises."

"Paris!" said Dad. "Just the two of us!" He looked over and winked at me.

"You mean for our anniversary?" said Mum, frowning. "But what about Sam and the shop and—"

"Rosy! It's only a week. Our first time away on our own since the girls were born. Bella can go to the cattery. Mags said Sam can stay with her *and* she's offered to keep an eye on the shop. I was going to tell you yesterday but you were so excited about the wedding and everything."

Mum started to smile. "Well, I have always dreamed about going to Paris," she said, clasping the tickets to her chest. "And I've been working so hard."

"So have I!" I complained. "But no one's whisking me off to Paris for a week!"

"Ahh, poor Sam," teased Dad. "Hey, aren't you finding out your parts at drama today?"

"Yeah, but I'm not expecting anything that

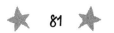

great," I said as casually as I could. "It's a brilliant show though. It's all about ghosts and phantom faces at the window."

"Well, just as long as you don't start letting your work slip," said Mum. "No big parts – remember?"

Dad shot her a look. "Come on, Rosy. It's Saturday, let her think about something apart from school for a few minutes at least!"

I gave Dad a grateful smile. Then I remembered the Great Wedding Clash and bit my lip.

"Hey, Mum, you know Sophia Malone's wedding, will you actually be going – you know, like *on* the day?"

"Of course," said Mum. "We'll be there all morning dressing the church and then they're going to whisk us off to some secret location to dress the tables. It's going to be a massive job. I might need your help actually. You'll have to miss drama that day if Mandy doesn't mind."

Missing drama was the least of my worries. What about missing Crystal's wedding?

I tried to call Crystal again on the way to drama. Where *was* she? Maybe the wedding invitation really was one big wind-up. That was just the sort of silly stunt she would pull. She'd do anything for a laugh, even if it left everyone else in a total tizz. I left her another message and hurried along the road to drama.

Ellie was waiting for me outside the hall.

"You'll never guess where I went yesterday after school," I said, giving her a quick hug. "But you mustn't tell a soul...do you swear?"

"Swear," she said, giggling. "Come on, tell."

I looked round to make sure no one was listening. "Adam's house!"

"Don't talk rubbish. *You went round to Adam's?*"

"Yes, but I'll tell you why later. Come on, let's go up, we're getting our parts today."

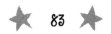

"Sam! You can't just say that and then stop – I'll go mad. Come on, give me a clue…"

"No clues," I said, running up the stairs. "I'll tell you later, I promise."

Adam was already in the hall when we got up there.

"Hi, Sam," he said, coming straight over.

"How's Riley?" I asked, trying very hard not to blush. I'd actually slapped on a load of extra-light face powder before I left the house to try and tone my cheeks down a bit.

"Gorgeous as ever. I gave him a great big kiss from you before I left this morning."

My face started to burn up. There was no way the powder could hide my blushes now. *Did he have to mention kissing?*

"Who's Riley?" said Ellie, her eyes so wide they were practically popping out of her head.

"We'd better go and find your bag," I muttered, grabbing her arm and steering her away from Adam.

"I haven't lost my bag!" she said, stumbling after me. "Did you fall on your head or something?"

"I fell on my head once," said Monty B, coming up from behind us. "I was trying to see what I looked like upside down in the mirror, but when I bent down to put my head between my legs I tipped right over."

"I want to know *everything*," hissed Ellie, ignoring Monty B. "Who's Riley? And what were you doing round at Adam's?"

But just then Mandy called us over.

"I've sorted out all the parts," she said, when we were sitting in a circle. "It wasn't easy and I've even had to add an extra character, but it's done and I'm happy so let's get on with it."

"I'll explain everything at Phoebe's," I whispered to Ellie. "You are still coming, aren't you?"

"Course."

I'd hardly thought about the show for days – my head had been so filled up with Crystal and the wedding. But I was still desperate to be Laura, whatever Mum thought about it. Mandy grabbed her folder from the piano and was about to read out the cast list when Arthur came bursting in, looking a bit frantic.

"I'm so sorry to interrupt you, Mandy," he said. "But I've lost something, you see, and it's vitally important it doesn't fall into the wrong hands."

"Oh dear, what is it? I didn't see anything when I arrived this morning."

"Maybe it's his breakfast," Ellie whispered. "Most of it seems to be in his beard."

"I can't actually say what it is," said Arthur. "It's very private, I'm afraid. But *please*, if you find anything at all that you think might belong to me, return it to my office as a matter of great urgency."

"It might help if we knew what we were

looking for..." Mandy started to say, but Arthur was already halfway out of the hall, muttering something to himself.

"Never a dull moment," said Mandy. "Now where were we?"

"You were just about to tell us about the extra part," said Phoebe.

"Oh yes. I decided to write in an extra part and it's for Sara..."

"*Me?*" said Sara, turning pink with excitement.

Mandy nodded, smiling. "Well, you were so good at acting Laura's part, I decided to add in a younger sister called Rianna. Laura and Ben's younger sister, if you see what I mean."

"You mean you wrote a part especially for *me*?"

Phoebe groaned. "I'll never hear the last of this," she said. "Couldn't she just be one of the servants or something?"

"I've got a *main* part, actually," said Sara,

"so why don't *you* go off and be one of the servants?"

"There's nothing wrong with being a servant," said Mandy, quickly. "*All* the parts are important, every single one."

"Oh, I know. It's just that Phoebe's such a pain. *Someone* has to put her in her place."

"I've been saying that for years," said Monty B.

"Shut up," said Phoebe, hitting him.

"Right," said Mandy. "So Sara is Rianna, Monty B, you're Mr. Biscuit the detective—"

"But I thought you said I wasn't allowed to be Mr. Biscuit," teased Monty B. "And that you were going to change his name."

"I know, I know, but you were so funny I can't really see anyone else doing it. But listen to me, Monty B, you have *got* to stick to the script!"

Monty B did a silly salute. "I swear on my life, Mandy. Stick to the script. That will be my mantra from this day forward. I don't mean stick to it like glue, obviously, because that would be stupid. Just stick to it word for word. Listen, I'll start right now. Stick to the script. Stick to the—"

Mandy held up her hand. "Enough!" she said. "We get it! Phoebe, you're Mr. Biscuit's assistant, Sugar, and Ellie, I'd like you to be Flora the castle cook and maid. Neesha, you've actually got two parts because you're the butler *and* the butler's identical twin brother."

"Oh my God, yeah, does that mean I'm the murderer?"

"Well, we're supposed to *think* it's a murder but in actual fact April has fallen in love and run off with the butler's identical twin."

I looked across at Adam. He was showing Catharine something in his script and she glanced up at him, smiling. She was always hanging around him at drama and I wondered if she fancied him as well. I dragged my eyes back to Neesha.

"So why is there a ghost at the window then, if she hasn't actually died?" she was saying.

"It's not real," said Mandy. "It's just April's face tormenting the butler from the past. That's why it's a phantom, not a ghost."

Neesha grinned. "I so don't have a clue what you're on about, Mandy, but it sounds wicked!"

"Now what about you, Sam?" Mandy looked over at me. "Who did you say you wanted to be again?"

I opened my mouth, and closed it again. I'd told her so many times. "W-what do you mean, *who do I want to be*?" I stammered. "I kept telling you, over and over. Don't you remember? I really—"

"I'm just kidding," she laughed. "Sam, you're going to be Laura, well done." She handed me a script, smiling.

"Yes!" I punched the air. "I'm Laura! I'm Laura!" I got up and did a little victory dance around Ellie.

"Where's Sandeep by the way?" said Mandy, frowning. "He hasn't rung me to say he couldn't make it today. Does anyone know?"

Just at that second we heard the downstairs door slam.

"That'll be him," I said, practically skipping round the hall in excitement. "Is he Ben? Is that what you were going to say? I've got to tell him."

I rushed over to the door, expecting to hear Sandeep's feet flying up the stairs, but there was nothing.

"Hang on a minute, what on earth was that?" said Mandy. There was a weird clunking noise. Someone was coming up the stairs, but it sounded as if they were dragging something very heavy behind them. *Clunk, drag, clunk, drag, clunk, drag...*

We all froze.

"Oh my God, yeah," said Neesha. "It sounds like something out of *Doctor Who*...or maybe it's the phantom face!"

But it wasn't a Dalek or a Cyberman or the face at the window.

It was Sandeep.

On crutches.

"Sorry I'm late," he panted, struggling to get through the door and completely out of breath. "I had a really bad accident at school and I've broken my leg."

We all unfroze. I held the door open while Mandy and Adam helped him into the hall and Ellie ran to grab a chair.

"Here, sit down," said Mandy. "What happened?"

Sandeep lowered himself down as carefully as he could. "Well, it's a bit embarrassing really, but basically I fell down the stairs. It was just that weird thing when you think there's another step there and then there isn't."

"The curse of the phantom step!" said Monty B and we all groaned.

"Did they have to call an ambulance?" said Sara. "I had to go in an ambulance once, didn't I, Phoebe?"

"This isn't really about you," said Phoebe.

"But you will still be able to be in the show, won't you?" I said.

Sandeep shook his head. "I don't think so. I mean I won't be able to get on and off the stage or anything like that. But I'd still like to come every week and help out with other stuff."

"Oh, Sandeep, there's heaps you could do!" cried Mandy, running her hands through her hair. "But you're right, it really wouldn't be safe to have you climbing on and off the stage. It's so old and there isn't even a proper rail to hold on to. I had cast you as Ben, I'm afraid, but I'll have to change things about a bit. Poor old Sandeep!"

"But I could help him, couldn't I?" I said desperately. "I'm really strong and he could sort of lean on me and there's no reason why he wouldn't be at a wedding in a castle with a broken leg, is there?"

"That's really nice of you, Sam," said Mandy, "but it just wouldn't be safe. Look, why don't you all have a game of Handshake Murder while I have a think about the show. Sandeep, you can choose the murderer and the detective."

Sandeep chose Neesha to be the detective and she went to stand outside.

I walked around the hall shaking hands with the others but staying as far away from Adam as I could. I didn't want to shake his hand and I really didn't want Mandy to choose him to be Ben instead of Sandeep. My hands started to feel hot and sweaty. Why on earth did Sandeep have to go and break his leg?

I stayed out of Adam's way for as long as

possible while everyone around me was dying. Eventually there was no getting away from him. He grabbed my hand and tickled my palm. He was the murderer. My face started to burn up. It was like an automatic response that I had no control over.

"Okay, come and sit down," Mandy called out from the front. "It's all sorted." Mandy read out the new cast list.

Adam was Ben.

I was dead!

"Come on then! Who's Riley?" Ellie demanded, the second we got up to Phoebe's room.

"Don't tell me you've got a boyfriend as well!" said Polly. "Is he cute?"

"Oh, he's *very* cute! The cutest thing you've ever seen in your life. He's got the deepest brown eyes and a very wet nose!"

Polly screwed up her face. "Ewww! What's the matter with him? Has he got a cold or something?"

"No, of course not," I said, laughing. "Riley is a puppy. One of Adam's puppies. My Aunty Mags is buying him. The puppy that is, not Adam."

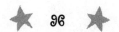

"So *that's* why you were round there," said Ellie. "I get it."

We all threw ourselves on Phoebe's bed, and began munching our way through a huge bowl of strawberries her mum had left for us.

"The thing is," I said, "I had no idea it was Adam's house. I was just sitting there with my aunt, cuddling this gorgeous little pup, when in he walks. I nearly had heart failure. He squashed right up next to me on the couch and everything. It was just so embarrassing."

Ellie sat up. "Hey, you know Adam and Eddie go to the same school, yeah, well Eddie told me that Adam really fancies someone at drama but he wouldn't tell me who it was. He said he was sworn to secrecy."

"No way," breathed Phoebe.

"I bet it's Sam," said Polly.

"Don't be stupid." My heart was pounding. Adam was in Year Ten – he wouldn't fancy someone in Year *Eight*, would he?

"Come on," Polly insisted. "He's always liked you, ever since the first show. It's so obvious."

"No it isn't," I said, burying my face in my script. "But wait till you see Riley, he's the most gorgeous, cute, adorable thing you've ever seen in your life. I just wish he was mine."

Suddenly Sara burst in to the room. "Talking about Adam again!" she said. "Oh Adam, you're the most gorgeous, cute, adorable thing I've ever seen in my life. I just wish you were mine!" She swooned onto the bed. "Can't I rehearse with you, *pleeease*? I'm bored to death downstairs by myself."

"No you can't! Get out!" said Phoebe. She pushed her off the end of the bed.

"And we weren't talking about Adam, we were talking about my aunt's new puppy!" I added.

"You don't have to be embarrassed about it, Sam," said Sara. "*Everyone* fancies Adam. And now Sandeep's broken his leg, you'll get to do all your scenes with him."

"What do you know about fancying boys?" said Ellie. "You're not even ten!"

Sara stood in the middle of the room, pouting. "I'm *nearly* ten *and* I'm getting hair extensions just like Mandy's – and anyway, I'm very grown up for my age, remember?"

"Oh, just go and watch TV or something," said Phoebe. "This is a private meeting and you have to be twelve or over to come in here."

Sara stamped her foot and flounced out of the room.

"See you in two years!" I shouted after her. "And I was *not* talking about ADAM! I honestly don't know how you put up with her, Phoebe," I said, turning back to the others. "I'm so happy *I* haven't got a little sister."

Phoebe laughed. "She's just jealous of you, Sam. She was desperate to be Laura and she knows you're the best at acting."

I shook my head, embarrassed. "No I'm not."

"Of course you are," she said. "By a mile."

"Seriously, Sam," said Polly. "I was round here the other day and we heard her in her room pretending that *you* had to leave Star Makers suddenly, and Mandy gave *her* your part. Right, Phoebs?"

Phoebe nodded. "It was totally sad! Oh, that reminds me actually," she said, jumping up. "You'll never guess who I saw yesterday, Sam. It was *your* sister, Crystal."

My mouth dropped open. "Don't be stupid."

"No really, we went to this market after school that my mum knows to get some material – it's a sort of arts and crafts market – and Crystal was there selling her jewellery. I'm pretty sure she didn't recognize me but it was definitely her. Look..."

She handed me a small card.

Crystal's Crystals
Hand-made silver jewellery
The perfect present — or why not treat yourself!

"Haven't you been there?" she babbled on. "It's such a cool place, and her stall was amazing. I really wanted to buy something myself but I didn't have enough money and Mum said she was broke."

"Oh, let's see," said Ellie, holding her hand out for the card. "I haven't seen your sister in ages, Sam. Has she been travelling or something?"

"She's moved in with her boyfriend," I mumbled, desperate to change the subject. It was so weird and kind of annoying to think of Crystal out there – merrily selling her jewellery – while I was worrying myself silly, waiting for her to call.

"Let's just start practising, can't we?" I said,

slipping the card into my pocket. I was fed up with Adam *and* Crystal. "Let's do the scene in Act Two when Mr. Biscuit questions everyone in the Grand Hall. We're *all* in that, even Flora the castle cook."

"What do you mean, *even* Flora the cook?" said Ellie. "My part's really good, if you don't mind." She grabbed her folder in a huff, but as she yanked it open, a scruffy, half-torn piece of paper covered in writing floated out from the centre of the script and down onto the bed in front of us.

We crowded round to see what it was and Ellie started reading out loud.

My darling,

I cannot keep my feelings trapped inside for one moment longer.

My heart yearns for you more each day. I'd like to think that over time you have grown to feel the same way, but please give me some sign,

some signal, that my love for you is not in vain.
I will watch and wait...
Forever yours, and I really do mean for ever...
Arthur

"Oh my giddy aunt!" said Ellie. "I think we've just found what Arthur was looking for."

We all stared at each other for a minute then collapsed back on the bed in hysterics. No wonder Arthur was in such a state. He'd written a love letter to Mandy and lost it.

"Oh my darling," spluttered Ellie, grabbing hold of me. "I cannot keep my feelings for you trapped inside for one moment longer. Give me some sign!"

"I can just imagine the sign Mandy would give Arthur, and it wouldn't be terribly loving," laughed Polly.

"I knew he liked her," I said. "It's been obvious for ages. The way he turns up every Saturday, thinking up a different reason to be there every time he comes in."

"What are we going to do with it, though? I mean it is very private. How do you think it ended up in your script in the first place?" Phoebe asked Ellie.

"I've got no idea," said Ellie. "You know what I'm like, I probably picked it up by mistake. Let's just take it back next Saturday and put it on the piano by Mandy's things – that way she can decide what to do with it." She caught my eye and made a stupid face and we started to laugh all over again.

"This is so nice – hanging out together. I'm glad you didn't meet up with Eddie this week," I said.

"He was a bit funny about it to tell you the truth," said Ellie, folding Arthur's letter and slipping it back in her script. "He said I shouldn't let you decide how I spend my Saturdays."

"Hey, that's not fair," said Polly. "Sam didn't decide. She just suggested we get together to practise the show. Why doesn't he join Star Makers if he's that bothered?"

I nodded, agreeing with Polly, but Ellie just sat there, looking confused. It was like Eddie was trying to come between us and she didn't even realize.

"Don't listen to him, Ellie," I said. "He's just being an idiot. We've been best friends for much longer than he's been around!"

"You're right," said Ellie quickly. "Friends First." But she didn't sound as if she meant it at all.

Phoebe rang Monty B to come over to join us and as soon as he arrived we began to practise the scene in the Grand Hall. It starts off quite serious. Mr. Biscuit is questioning each character about the face at the window, but then Ellie comes in with one of those old-fashioned silver trolleys to serve tea.

"Oh splendid!" says Monty B. "There's nothing like a cup of tea to help things along."

Ellie hands Monty B one of those dainty little teacups and says, "Biscuit?" and he says, "It's *Mr.* Biscuit, if you don't mind!" But of course she's got no idea that his *name* is Mr. Biscuit, so she just gives him this really funny look, holds out the plate of biscuits and says, "Oh, I am sorry, Sir, would you like a *Mr.* Biscuit, Sir?" and Phoebe says, "No, no, *he's* Mr. Biscuit," and Ellie says, "Oh I understand," not understanding at all, and says, "Would you like a *Mr.* Biscuit, Mr. Biscuit?" and it goes on and on like that, getting more and more ridiculous.

"I'll never be able to do this onstage without laughing," said Ellie. "You know what I'm like once I start giggling. And stop making that funny face, Monty B!"

"He's not," said Phoebe. "That's just the way he looks!"

"Thanks a lot!" said Monty B, and we all cracked up again. It was the best time I'd had in ages. I loved the new show and I loved being round at Phoebe's having such a giggle with everyone.

When I got home I slipped Crystal's little card into the envelope with the invitation and the note. Something else to hide from Mum. The invitation, my part in the show and now this. I used to think that families shouldn't be allowed to keep secrets from each other, that there should be some law against it or something, but here I was, keeping so many secrets from Mum I was in danger of bursting at any moment.

I lay down on my bed, the envelope safe under my pillow. If Crystal didn't call me soon, or come and see me at school...well, I would just have to go and find her myself.

Could Things Get Any More Embarrassing Than This?!

8

As soon as we got to drama the next Saturday, Phoebe, Polly and I made a sort of barrier around Ellie while she slipped Arthur's letter onto the piano by Mandy's things. It was all my idea of course and it worked brilliantly. Mandy was busy talking to one of the parents, so she definitely didn't see what we were up to. It was impossible to concentrate after that though. Every time she went anywhere near the piano we all held our breath, waiting to see what would happen – but then she'd pick up a pen or grab her script and not even notice the letter at all.

Just before break she called us over to the piano to teach us the second song in the show,

"Clueless". She picked up the music and was just about to sit down when she finally spotted the scruffy piece of paper. The others carried on chatting, waiting for her to start playing but the four of us froze, our eyes fixed firmly on her face as she read Arthur's love letter.

Her eyes opened wider and wider and her mouth went all twitchy at the corners, as if she was trying very hard not to laugh. I had to breathe really deeply not to burst out laughing myself and I didn't dare look over at Ellie. When Mandy finished reading, she stood there for a minute, biting her lip, then she folded the letter up and put it inside her bag.

"Okay," she said. "Let's make a start."

"I really hope Arthur comes in later," whispered Polly. "I can't wait to see what she says."

"Or what sign she gives him," I whispered back and I had to bury my face in my script to stop myself snorting.

"Clueless" is the song Monty B and Phoebe sing when they arrive at the castle to solve the mystery of the phantom face – but the point of the song is that they really don't have a clue about anything. Monty B comes onstage with this massive magnifying glass, as if he's searching for evidence, and Phoebe follows on behind with a pen and a little book, ready to make a note of anything he finds.

They sing the first part of the song by themselves as they arrive, and then the rest of us join in with the second chorus.

I'm Biscuit! I'm Sugar!
And we're here to sort out this mystery from the past
And though we're not terribly quick or especially fast
We won't leave this place
Or the strange phantom face
Till we find out what happened

And sort out this case at last.

We don't have a clue, it's true
But wait till this case is through
We're clueless, its true, right now
But wait till we take our bow!

We don't have a clue, it's true
But wait till this case is through
We don't have a clue right now
But please let us take a bow!

Phoebe is brilliant at singing and Monty B's just got one of those faces that makes you laugh even when he's not trying to be funny. They'd obviously practised it together during the week because they'd added all these hilarious, slapstick actions, and at one point Mandy had to stop playing the piano, she was laughing so much.

"Oh my goodness, it's perfect casting," she

said, wiping her eyes. "Just don't get too carried away, will you, Monty B?"

"Stick to the script!" said Monty B, saluting.

When we'd learned the chorus and sung it through a few times, Mandy sent us off in groups to practise the scene leading up to the song. I had to team up with Adam and Sara, worse luck. I tried to get Sara on her own to warn her not to say anything stupid about me and Adam, but Adam came straight over before I could talk to her.

"Look after Sara, would you, Sam?" said Mandy as we clambered onto the stage to get away from the others. "It is her first production, don't forget."

"And her last with any luck!" I muttered to myself.

Adam was wearing his black beanie hat and black Dr. Martens boots and he looked so cool I had to force myself not to stare at him. I kept thinking about what Eddie said, about Adam liking someone at drama, and I couldn't help wondering if Polly was right and it might be me after all.

"You wouldn't believe how much Riley has grown," he said to me as we grabbed some chairs and sat down. "I think my mum's going to ring your aunt at some point today to let her know she can come and pick him up this afternoon. Why don't you come with her and we can go over some of our scenes together?"

"Oh, I've heard *all* about Riley," said Sara. I shot her a look. "Oh, he's just the most gorgeous, cute, adorable thing that I've ever seen in my life! That's what you said the other day, wasn't it, Sam? Or maybe you weren't talking about *Riley* at all?" She snorted into her script.

"Drop it, Sara. Let's just do the scene. Mandy's going to come over in a minute." I put my hands up to my cheeks to try and cool them down. I was going to kill Sara later. She might be jealous of me but I wish she'd just keep her mouth shut. And there was no way I was going back round to Adam's. There was a limit to the amount of times I was willing to make an idiot of myself.

We had a go at setting the scene ourselves and were just in the middle of showing Mandy what we'd done when Arthur came in.

"All hard at work," he boomed. "That's what I like to see."

"Is everything okay?" said Mandy, blushing a bit.

"Couldn't be better," said Arthur.

He didn't say anything else for a minute and neither did Mandy.

"So…" she said in the end, prompting him to get on with it.

"So…the thing is, Mandy my dear, I was just wondering if I might ask you something… ahem…in private."

Mandy started to blush even more. "I'm

sorry, Arthur, but I can't just walk out and leave the children."

"Oh, not to worry," said Arthur, backing out of the room. "I'll catch you later on, if I may. It won't take a second."

He swung round and swooped out of the room, his funny black cape flying out behind him. Mandy just stood there, staring at the door. She was probably trying to work out how quickly she could escape at the end of the session. I looked over at Ellie and she raised her eyebrows, grinning.

We couldn't talk about Arthur or the letter at break because Monty B, Catharine and Neesha were sitting with us. Sara was sitting on the other side of the hall with Tara – the further away the better as far as I was concerned – and Adam was helping Sandeep sort out a game for later on in the session.

"Don't forget you're coming out with Eddie today," said Ellie. "What do you feel like doing?"

I shrugged, shaking my head. I didn't feel like doing anything, not with Eddie.

"Are you guys coming as well?" she asked Polly and Phoebe. "We could go up to the shopping centre if you want."

"I can't," said Phoebe, "not unless you want Sara tagging along."

"Why does your mum keep getting you to look after her?" said Polly.

Phoebe sighed. "It's difficult, you know, because my dad always goes to his meditation centre on Saturday afternoons, so if Mum goes to work someone has to stay in and look after Sara."

"Well, I'll come over to yours if you want, Sugar, my sweet," said Monty B. "We can practise our song and some of our scenes."

"That sounds fun. I'll come too," I said quickly.

"No you won't," said Ellie, jutting her chin out. "A deal's a deal."

After break we sang the opening number and then put all the scenes together leading up to "Clueless". I tried really hard not to let the fact that I was onstage with Adam affect my performance. My voice did wobble a few times and my heart was racing, but Laura has to sound slightly scared about the face at the window anyway so it didn't really matter. I mean if you're serious about acting, you can't let a little thing like acting with a drop-dead gorgeous Year Ten boy put you off!

We finished the session with Sandeep's game. He'd written out a list of ten forfeits and Mandy divided us up into four teams. Each team had a copy of the forfeits and a pile of numbers from "1" to "10".

I was in team four and so was Ellie, but the others in our team were Neesha, Adam and Sara! I knew Adam would be on my team before Mandy even called out the numbers. I was doomed!

I looked down at the list of forfeits.

1. Ask someone in the room to marry you.
2. Say the alphabet backwards.
3. Run round the hall on someone's back. Well, they run — you just hang on for dear life!
4. Shake hands with three people in another team.
5. Shuffle round the hall on your bum three times.
6. Sing "Happy Birthday" in a very high voice.
7. Choose a nursery rhyme and sing it while holding your nose and standing on one leg.
8. Leapfrog over three people.
9. Count backwards from 100 to 1.
10. Tell everyone in your group that you love them — one at a time.

NO WAY. I couldn't play a game like this with Adam. Some of the tasks were so embarrassing I felt dizzy just reading them. I decided to disappear into the loo until the end of the session. I started to edge towards the door, but before I could make my escape Adam grabbed my arm and pulled me over to where the rest of the team were waiting.

Sandeep explained that we had to take turns to run into the middle, pick up a number from our pile, run back to our team and perform the task that matched the number. The first team to finish all their numbers was the winner.

I volunteered to go first – just to get it over with! I ran into the middle of the hall, praying I wouldn't pick anything too awful.

"WHAT NUMBER? WHAT NUMBER?" Adam shouted, as I dashed back to my team.

I looked down at my scrap of paper. "Erm... three."

He scanned the sheet of tasks.

"Quick! Jump on my back, Sam! You've got to go round the hall on someone's back and I'm the strongest."

He bent down, and I just about managed to clamber onto his back with a bit of help from Neesha and Ellie. It all happened so fast I didn't have time to think about how embarrassing it was.

"Don't drop me!" I shrieked, and then held on for dear life as Adam tore round the hall, trying not to bump into anyone. On the way we passed Catharine, who was shuffling around on her bum, and Monty B proposing to Phoebe!

My next turn was even worse. I picked up number ten, which meant I had to tell everyone in my group I loved them – one by one. I could feel the blood rush to my face as I mumbled "I love you" to Ellie, Neesha, Sara and – *Oh My God* – Adam!

"Speak up, Sam," said Sara. "I can hardly hear you!"

I forced the words out through my teeth *again* and collapsed down next to Ellie. Drama had turned into the biggest nightmare since Mandy decided to let Sara join – and since my *hormones had gone haywire*. It's like I was on automatic pilot. I only had to think about Adam and my face turned beetroot, and there didn't seem to be anything I could do about it!

"Hey, it's a shame Arthur's not playing," said Ellie. "He could declare his undying love for Mandy! He could even propose!" Then she leaped up ready for her turn, crashing into Adam, who had run back with number one and was making a big show of proposing to Neesha. It's just as well he didn't propose to me, because there's no way I would've said yes, not in a billion years.

When we went downstairs at the end of the session, Arthur was waiting for Mandy, Eddie was waiting for Ellie, and Aunty Mags was waiting for me.

"Come on! We're going to get Riley!" she cried, grabbing me and pulling me towards the

car. "Adam's mum called me this morning and it's all been arranged. We've just got to pop to the pet shop and make sure we've got everything we need and then we'll head straight over."

I looked across at Eddie, smirking at me from under his baseball cap, and I decided very quickly that a visit to Adam's, however embarrassing, would be better than spending the whole afternoon with Ellie and Eddie. He was starting to give me the creeps, big time. I explained to Ellie and gave her a quick hug. She wasn't happy, but at least she could see I had a real excuse.

"I'll see you a bit later then, Sam," said Adam. "And bring your script."

I nodded and mumbled something pathetic.

Mandy was parked right by Aunty Mags and the last thing I heard her say to Arthur before we drove off was that he'd have to catch her another time because she had an urgent appointment – at the dentist!

The
Big Row!

Aunty Mags was *so* excited about picking up Riley. She went on and on about it all the way to the pet shop and then all the way to Adam's house. I didn't pay much attention, to be honest. I was far too busy trying to work out how to keep my cool round at Adam's without sticking a great big ice pack on my face.

I knew we were only going to pick up Riley and that it was no big deal, but I couldn't stop thinking about how Adam had more or less invited me over, and not just because of Riley, but to *practise our scenes together*. While Aunty Mags went on about dog food and baskets and how to get rid of fleas, I went over everything that had happened this term at Star Makers, and in the end I was more or less convinced that the person Eddie was talking about when he said Adam liked someone at drama might actually be ME!

"Earth to Sam!" said Aunty Mags, pulling up outside Adam's house. "You're not listening to a single word. What's so interesting?"

"Oh nothing," I said. "It's just that...do you think when someone says that someone likes someone, but you don't actually know who that someone is, that that someone could be someone who's quite a bit younger than the someone who likes them?"

Aunty Mags turned to face me. "Are you feeling okay?" she said, touching my forehead. "I didn't understand a word of that!"

"Oh, it doesn't matter," I mumbled. "Come on, let's go in."

We could hear the puppies yapping before we even rang the bell, and when Mrs. Dale opened the door they literally threw themselves at us.

"Oh, they've grown loads!" cried Aunty Mags, kneeling down. The puppies clambered and climbed all over her, licking and nipping. "Look, Sam, here's Riley," she said, picking up the smallest pup – but I wasn't there to see Riley.

"Where's Adam?" I asked, peering over Mrs. Dale's shoulder. "We're supposed to be practising our scenes together." So much for being cool!

"Oh, he was straight in and straight out after drama," said Mrs. Dale. "Off to see a film with Catharine from Star Makers – some last-minute arrangement. He said he's sorry and he'll see you at drama next week. She's a lovely girl, but I never see him these days!"

I kneeled down to stroke Riley, just to give myself something to do. I didn't get it. Why would he ask me over to practise our scenes together but then go out with Catharine instead? It didn't make any sense – unless the girl Eddie was talking about when he said Adam fancied someone at drama was Catharine. I carried on stroking Riley, blinking back tears, hoping Mrs. Dale and Aunty Mags wouldn't notice how upset I was.

Mrs. Dale offered us tea, but Aunty Mags was bursting to get back home with Riley – and I certainly didn't want to hang about.

Riley sat in the back of the car in the little dog-carrier we'd bought at the pet shop. He whimpered the whole way, confused about leaving his mum and the other pups.

"Poor little thing," soothed Aunty Mags. "Wait until you see where you're going to live. You'll soon feel at home. Are you going to come over, Sam? Help settle him in?"

"Not today, Aunty Mags. Can you take me straight home? I've got heaps of homework."

"You're ever so quiet. You're not worried about anything, are you?"

"No, nothing important. It's just that I don't

understand why people say things they don't mean."

"You're talking in riddles again, sweetheart. Who's said something?"

I shrugged. "Oh, forget it. It's stupid anyway."

Dad was watching TV when I got in – some ancient black-and-white movie on BBC2.

"This is such a classic, Sam," he said, moving up to make room for me on the sofa.

"I'm not in the mood," I muttered. The way I was feeling, the last thing I wanted to do was sit through one of those old romantic films. "Anyway, I've got tons of work to do and I can't let my marks slip!" I added sarcastically.

Dad turned the volume down. "Don't be like that." He patted the couch. "Come and sit with your old dad for a sec. How did Mags get on with the puppy?"

"He's called Riley and he's gorgeous. But seriously, Dad, I've got to go and start my homework."

Dad jumped up suddenly and grabbed the remote, singing into it like it was a microphone. *"How much is that doggy in the window? The one with the waggly tail..."*

"*Dad!*" I knew he was trying to cheer me up, but it wasn't going to work. Not today. I edged past him and escaped upstairs to text Ellie.

Need 2 talk right now! Call me!

I lay on my bed waiting, but she didn't call back. She sent me this stupid picture of her and Eddie instead – their faces all squashed together, grinning at the camera. She'd only known him for about a month but he was already more important to her than her best friend. I wanted to tell her about Adam, to ask what Eddie meant when he said Adam fancied someone at drama. It had to be Catharine. Or else it was one big wind-up. Eddie's idea of a joke. A minute later another picture popped up on my phone, but this one was from Aunty Mags. It was the most gorgeous photo of Riley cuddled up in his basket, with the message: *True Love...*

I wondered if Ellie was in love with Eddie, or if it was just her hormones. I didn't actually trust Eddie one little bit. I couldn't shake the feeling that he was trying to turn Ellie against me, and it was really starting to get on my nerves. Before Ellie went on holiday, whenever we talked about what it would be like to have a boyfriend she was always the one to say friends come first. She'd obviously forgotten all about that quickly enough. It was more like *hello Eddie...goodbye Sam!*

At lunch on Monday, she was doing her usual routine of recounting every last juicy detail of her Saturday afternoon with Eddie – where they'd been and what he'd said and how cute he was. Polly and Phoebe just sat there like lemons listening to every word as if it was the most fascinating thing they'd ever heard in their lives.

"Stop going on about him all the time, can't you?" I said when she finally paused for breath. "I don't know what you think is so great about him anyway. He's such a creep."

She whipped round to face me. "Shut up, Sam. No he isn't. You're just jealous."

"No I'm not. He just wants you to think that so you hang around with *him* instead of me. It's so obvious, you'd have to be stupid not to realize!"

"So you're calling me stupid now, are you?" she shouted. "Some friend you've turned out to be." Her eyes filled with tears.

I shook my head, frustrated that she didn't get it. "I'm not calling you stupid. I'm just trying to warn you."

"*Warn* me? I don't *need* warning, thanks very much. You're the one I need to stay away from, not Eddie!" She wiped her eyes on her sleeve and stormed out of the canteen.

Phoebe and Polly sat there with their mouths wide open.

"Go after her," said Phoebe. "She's really upset. Go and say sorry, quickly!"

"Why should I?" I said stubbornly. "She'll soon realize I'm right when she thinks about it. She won't stay angry for long."

But she did stay angry – all that day and the next and the day after. She didn't speak to me all week and it was awful. She didn't sit with me at lunch or wait for me after classes or anything. It was like being stuck in a nightmare where everything's going wrong but you can't make yourself wake up. I kept trying to catch her eye – and a couple of times I waited for her outside class – but she just swept straight past me as if I was invisible. It began to feel as if we'd never been friends in the first place.

Phoebe tried to talk to her but she wouldn't

listen. She said I was jealous and spiteful and she didn't want anything to do with me.

"Just tell her you're really, really sorry," said Phoebe.

"It shouldn't be me saying sorry, she's the one who's dropped me the second Eddie came along."

"Well, she didn't *drop* you exactly," said Polly. "I mean she did keep asking you to go with them on Saturdays after drama."

"I know, but you don't understand."

Neither of them understood. They didn't realize how much I missed my Saturday afternoons with Ellie. Or how much I wanted to talk to her about Adam, and Crystal, and the two weddings, and everything else that was going on.

By Friday it felt as if we hadn't been talking for years. I tried one last time to catch her as she was going into lunch, but it was useless.

"Come on, Ellie," I said, grabbing her arm.

"This is stupid. How long are you going to keep this up? I was only trying to help."

She shook my hand off and pushed past me. "I know you think I'm stupid," she said. "You've told me enough times. But I don't care any more!"

"Fine!" I shouted after her. "Have a nice time with *Eddie*, because I don't care any more either!"

I trailed out of school at the end of the day feeling totally fed up. It's usually the happiest time of the week. We all spill out together, excited about the weekend, and especially excited about Star Makers, but I didn't even know where Ellie was. I hung about outside the gates waiting to see if she would turn up. I knew it wouldn't do any good, but I just wanted to see her.

A minute later I noticed a tall blonde girl walking straight towards me from down the road. Her hair was backcombed and wild like a massive haystack, and she was wearing the skinniest black jeans with heavy, black Dr. Martens boots.

I couldn't believe it. *Finally*. I took a step towards her, grinning.

"Hello, gorgeous," she said, holding her arms out.

It was Crystal.

And I was *so* relieved to see her I didn't know whether to laugh or cry.

A Drama at Drama!

10

"Crystal!!!" I flew into her arms, half-laughing, half-crying.

"What a welcome!" Crystal hugged me close and then pushed me away to look at me. "Hey! You're not getting snot all over my T-shirt, are you? Why so sad, Sam? What's going on?"

"What's going on?" I squealed, beating her chest. "Where have you been? Why haven't you been returning my calls? I got the invitation and then nothing. I've been going mad."

She pulled me back into her arms. "I'm sorry," she said into my hair. "It's just been crazy; the wedding and the business and Tyler's music. I haven't had a second to think about anything else. I should've called, I know, but hey! I'm here now."

She hugged me one more time, then grabbed my arm and started pulling me down the street.

"Come on, you old slowcoach. You don't want to hang about school on a Friday afternoon. Let's go down to the park. I've got so much to tell you." She was half-running, shouting at the top of her voice, her eyes wild with excitement. I ran along with her, caught up in the moment – caught up in her crazy mood – just like always.

There's a small playground a few streets away from school and we flew in through the entrance, out of breath and laughing.

"Hey, I've got something to ask you," she said, as we collapsed down on the big-kid swings to get our breath back. "Why were you standing outside school by yourself? Who were you waiting for? I haven't ruined some hot date, have I?"

"Don't be stupid!" I said. "I've had a massive row with Ellie. That's why I was by myself. I was standing there like an idiot hoping she might show up so we could sort things out, but it's hopeless."

"Oh Sam, not you and Ellie." She reached across and linked her arm through mine. "What did you fight about? It wasn't a boy, was it?"

"How did you guess?" I said, half-smiling. "It *was* about a boy, but it wasn't really my fault. You see Ellie met this awful guy Eddie on holiday. She says he's not her boyfriend but they keep hanging out together all the time. She sees him more or less *every* Saturday, and honestly, Crystal, he's such a creep."

"Nightmare!" said Crystal.

"I know, and that's not all," I said, the words tumbling out. "You see I kind of like Adam at drama – you know, he was my husband in *The Dream Factory* – and he kind of asked me over to practise our scenes together at his house, but when I got there his mum said he'd gone out with *Catharine* from drama. So now I'm thinking he doesn't even know I exist. I mean, I might as well be invisible. I probably am to him."

"*What, you? Invisible?!*" cried Crystal. "Impossible!" Then she jumped off her swing and plonked herself down on my lap. "Oh sorry," she said, leaping up, "I didn't realize anyone was sitting there."

"Shut up!" I said, but we were both laughing.

We swung back and forth for ages, our feet trailing on the ground. Crystal filled me in on how well her jewellery was selling and described all the new pieces she'd been working on. Her arms were jangling with some bangles she'd just made, thin silver circles with shiny crystals embedded into the metal. She was full of exciting ideas. She was going to make brooches and mirrors, and candleholders with crystals dotted around the rim.

She told me about her flat, and about Tyler and The Garlic Pickers and how well their gigs were going. She barely paused for breath as she raced from one topic to another.

"They're actually about to get some big news, and I mean really BIG! But I can't tell you what it is because I've been sworn to secrecy." She zipped her mouth shut.

"What, you mean like a recording contract or something?"

"Seriously, I can't say. We don't know all the details yet anyway, but when we find out you'll be the first to know, Sam, promise!"

She went on and on, telling me about all the different markets she worked at and how weird it was to do her own washing and cooking. She laughed hysterically at some of the disasters she'd had, like forgetting about her bath running until the water started dripping through the neighbours' ceiling, and how she'd burned the dinner so badly she'd had to throw the pans straight into the bin. The only thing she didn't talk about was the wedding.

I knew I should tell her that Mum was doing the flowers for Sophia Malone's wedding on the same day as *her* wedding, but I didn't know how to bring it up.

"What about you and Mum?" I said in the end, when she finally stopped for a second. "When are you going to tell her and Dad about you and Tyler getting married?"

Crystal stopped laughing. Her face closed up and she pulled her arm away.

"I don't want to talk about Mum."

"But you've got to, Crystal. The wedding's in *six weeks*. You can't get married without telling Mum. And what about Dad...and Aunty Mags?"

"I don't know what to do about Dad," she said quietly. "He's just got stuck in the middle of this mess with Mum."

 140

"But what is the mess? Why won't anyone tell me? Is it something to do with what Mum said to you at your party that night?"

Crystal leaped up from the swing and turned to face me.

"That night was supposed to be special," she said. "It was my eighteenth birthday. All my friends were there. It was *my* night."

"I know and it was brilliant. I was there, remember?"

"Yes, but you weren't there at the end when Mum and I had our little chat, were you? You weren't there when I told Mum I wasn't taking up my place at uni."

Her eyes were glistening with tears. "Come on, we'd better be getting back." She pulled me up off the swing and started walking out of the park, striding ahead in her big black boots.

"But what did she say?" I said, running to catch up. "How bad could it be? Can't you sort it out?"

Crystal turned back towards me, sighing. "It's not some little row over a boy like you and Ellie. It's serious, Sam, and it's up to Mum to sort it out, not me. I do want to invite them to the wedding but I can't – not until Mum faces up to what she's done."

We walked back in silence. The sky was full of heavy black clouds as if a storm was brewing. I wanted to ask her what Mum was supposed to be facing up to and how she expected me to keep such a big secret. I wanted to know where she was living and why she didn't call me more often, but her mood had changed. It was heavy and black like the clouds and I didn't know how she'd react if I started asking her a whole load of questions.

"Hey, Crystal – *you* remember when I used to dress up as Sam from *Green Eggs and Ham*, don't you?" was all I managed in the end. We were almost home, about to go our separate ways.

"Course I do," she said. "How could I *ever* forget that little red hat?" She hugged me tightly. "I love you, Sam Lester!"

"I love you too," I mumbled into her shoulder – and then a second later she was gone.

I dragged myself out of bed the next morning after the worst night. I was actually dreading Star Makers for the first time ever. It was bad enough Ellie not speaking to me at school, but it was going to be even worse at drama. I was literally bursting to tell her about Crystal turning up, and the wedding dilemma – I could just imagine her face – but when I got there she wouldn't even meet my eye, let alone talk to me. And then there was Adam. I was planning to stay right out of his way, but he came straight over the second I walked in.

"Hi, Sam, how's Riley getting on? I've missed him like crazy, you know!"

"I haven't seen him," I said as airily as I could, even though my heart was racing at a hundred miles an hour. I half wanted to ask him why he'd gone out that day – and whether he actually fancied Catharine – but even if I'd had the guts, I didn't really want to hear the answers.

As soon as everyone had arrived, Mandy got us up onstage to practise the scene where Monty B and Phoebe discuss the clues they've found around the castle. Ellie comes on halfway through to serve tea to everyone, but as she went round each of the characters she purposely left me out.

"That's a bit babyish, isn't it?" I said, totally fed up with the whole situation.

"Not as babyish as you warning me to stay away from Eddie!" she shot back.

"Hang on a sec!" said Monty B. "That's not in the script, is it? I thought I was the only one who made things up around here!"

"Oh, Sam's the expert at making things up!" said Ellie. "Everything she says is a load of made-up rubbish."

"Speak up, guys!" said Sandeep suddenly. He was sitting at the back of the hall to make sure we were projecting our voices properly.

"She said, *Sam's the expert at making things up!*" Sara shouted at the top of her voice. "And that *everything she says is a load of made-up rubbish!*"

"Shut up!" I snapped.

"What's going on?" said Mandy. "Can we just get on with the scene?"

Monty B walked over to the edge of the stage. "Now I know I'm only a fictional detective called Biscuit, but using all the clues I've gathered in the last two and a half minutes I'd say that Sam and Ellie aren't talking because Sam made something up about Ellie and her new boyfriend Eddie. How impressive is that?"

"You can shut up as well!" I said to Monty B.

"Sam, can you please stop telling everyone to shut up," said Mandy.

"Oh my God, yeah," said Neesha. "This is like one of those documentaries on TV when they follow a group putting on a show. You know, like A Drama Within a Drama! Whatever happens, someone *always* runs out in tears."

"Seriously, Sam," said Mandy, "if you've had a row with Ellie, sort it out later."

"I don't want to sort it out," I muttered. "She's the one who's turned it into some big thing!"

Ellie rounded on me, furious. "If you were a real friend you'd be happy for me," she yelled. "Eddie was right! It's just because you weren't the first one to have a boyfriend!" She folded her arms, challenging me to disagree.

"I thought you said he was *just a friend*," I taunted. "And anyway, I don't want a boyfriend, thanks very much."

"What? Not even that most gorgeous, cute and adorable boy you like at drama?" said Sara in an even louder voice than before. "Not that I'd ever say who it was," she added, staring right at Adam.

"Girls!" snapped Mandy. "That's enough! If you can't get on with each other, come off the stage." I didn't need asking twice. I gave Ellie *and* Sara the most evil look I could muster and stormed off the stage and out of the hall.

"Told you!" I heard Neesha call out behind me. "Someone *always* runs out in tears."

I wasn't in tears but I was close. Everything was going wrong. Crystal was getting married to Tyler in secret. Sara kept embarrassing me in front of Adam – as if I wasn't embarrassed enough already – and Ellie was treating me like I was her worst enemy. I couldn't believe our friendship was over. She probably thought I didn't care but I did – more than anything.

11
Even More Secrets!

I'd switched off my phone so it didn't ring during drama but when I turned it back on there was a message from Mum asking me to come straight down to *Everything's Rosy*. I rushed along the high street, thinking about Ellie and how angry she was. I suppose it was true that I hadn't really given Eddie a chance, but I didn't get why he kept saying things about me and why Ellie was so ready to believe him. Maybe our friendship wasn't as strong or as special as I'd always thought it was.

As soon as I walked into *Everything's Rosy* I started to feel a bit better. It's like stumbling across a secret hideaway full of hidden treasure. It's crammed full of frosted-glass vases, each one packed with brightly-coloured exotic flowers. Ivies trail out of hand-made plant boxes and there are reams of fancy ribbons for tying bouquets. But most amazing of all is the smell; a gorgeous mix of all the different flowers and the big scented candles that burn slowly throughout the day.

"Thank heavens you're here, Sam," said Mum, emerging from her office at the back as the front-door bell jingled behind me. "Myra and Keeley both called in sick. Can you believe it? On a *Saturday*! I'm literally drowning in orders. You couldn't give me a hand, could you?"

I dumped my bag in the back and got straight to work. I'd learned how to arrange flowers years ago when Mum was starting out. Crystal would come in to help out at the weekends and I'd tag along, desperate to keep up with whatever she was doing.

I knew how to choose the colours so they

matched and how to bulk out the orders with delicate ferns and sprays of shiny viburnum. Once I'd done that, Mum would trim them down and wrap them up. She could transform a simple bunch of flowers into the most beautiful bouquet in seconds.

We didn't really talk – there was far too much to do. I didn't feel much like talking anyway. I couldn't tell her about drama because I'd only end up blabbing about my part – and I didn't know how to talk to her about Crystal without her going off the deep end. We worked right through the orders, only stopping when a customer came in or the phone rang. It was nearly four when the van was finally loaded up and ready to take the last deliveries.

Mum slumped against the door, groaning. "You're a lifesaver, Sam! Thanks so much for helping."

"That's okay. I'll just go and grab my things."

"You wouldn't have a quick look at some of the designs I've done for the wedding before you go, would you?" she said. "It'll only take a few minutes."

We squashed into her little office at the back and she poured me a cup of tea.

"Sophia can't seem to make her mind up about what she's after, so Lavender, the wedding planner, keeps ringing me every five minutes with some *great* new idea. It's all '*Oh darling!*' this and '*Oh darling!*' that. I've never done a job like it before – it's crazy."

"Come on then, *darling*," I joked. "Show me what you've done. Is she *really* called Lavender?"

Mum nodded, rolling her eyes. She opened a big sketchbook and I sipped my tea, relaxing properly for the first time all day.

"I haven't actually decided on anything yet," she said, looking a bit worried. "I've come up with a few ideas but I'm not sure they're very good. You know me, I don't have any problem with the business side of things, but I'm not so confident about the really artistic stuff."

"You need Crystal for that!" I blurted out. "She's the creative one!"

Mum snapped the book shut, her hands trembling suddenly.

"I'm just saying, you know, because she's so good at that sort of thing and I saw her yesterday and her jewellery designs are so beautiful..." I trailed off.

Mum's eyes narrowed. "What do you mean, you saw her yesterday? You didn't tell me? Where did you see her? I thought I made it clear that I don't want you going round to that flat of hers."

"*Mum!* I didn't go to her flat. I don't even know where it is. What are you going to say next – that I'm not allowed to see my own sister? How long is this going to carry on?" I scraped my chair back and flounced out of the office. It was like living in the middle of a war zone, but Mum and Crystal were both so stubborn that there was no getting through to either of them.

Mum followed me out of the office. "Well, thanks for helping," she said tightly. Her eyes were bright and I could tell she was trying not to cry. "You'd better get off now – I'm sure you've got lots of homework."

I breathed in, clenching my fists. I felt like saying, *I have, I've got tons, but I'm not doing any of it until you and Crystal make up*. I know it was immature but, seriously, how did she think I was supposed to concentrate on my homework when all this other family stuff was going on? If my grades started to slip, it wouldn't be because I had a big part at drama.

I stomped off towards home, furious. Mum couldn't stop me seeing my own sister – and when was she going to admit how much she was missing Crystal herself? I was almost back when I saw Aunty Mags coming towards me from the opposite direction. She had Riley with her on the lead, wriggling and squirming all over the place.

"It's his first proper walk, Sam," she called out, waving. "Why don't you come down to the park with us?"

Riley loved the park. There were so many new smells that he went crazy sniffing his way around the grass in a total frenzy, pulling Aunty Mags after him.

"As soon as he's old enough he's going straight to obedience classes," she said. "He's already chewed half the house to bits!"

"I bet that's what Mum would like to do," I said glumly, "send *me* to obedience classes."

Aunty Mags burst out laughing. "Oh come on, Sam, it's not as bad as all that, is it?"

"I just wish she'd make up with Crystal – but even more than that, I wish she's realize how important acting is to me. I've got one of the biggest parts in the show, but I can't even tell her. She's already warned me that if I have too many lines to learn she'll stop me going."

"Oh Sam, I know she wants you to do well at school, but I'm sure she wouldn't go as far as that."

"It's true, Aunty Mags. She's been on at me about it ever since Crystal left. She's even threatened to get me a tutor on Saturday mornings and I love going to Star Makers more than anything. Well, I did until I started *this* show. You wouldn't believe what happened this morning, it was a nightmare." I told her all about rowing with Ellie – and Sara embarrassing me in front of everyone – and how difficult it was to act with Adam.

"The awful thing is I'm a bit like Sara myself," I admitted. "Always shooting my mouth off and thinking I'm the bees knees! I don't even know if I can face going back, to tell you the truth."

"No, you must!" cried Aunty Mags. "And I'm going to come and watch you and I'll cheer so loud they'll hear me in the next town. You're nearly thirteen, Sam, you're going to get all sorts of crushes on boys. You can't give up your drama club just because you *like* someone. And anyway, I thought you were serious about being an actress?"

"Stop it! I am!"

The crazy thing was I quite liked it when Aunty Mags gave me advice. I don't know why, but it made me feel special. It was the way she listened to everything I said; I mean *really* listened. I don't remember anyone ever listening to me like that before. Certainly not Mum, Dad was always working, and Crystal was so full of her own news she didn't always have the patience to listen to mine.

"Look, let's sit down for a bit," said Aunty Mags, pulling me towards a bench. "Riley looks as if he needs a rest." She picked up Riley and plonked him on her lap. "Seriously, Sam, if you think your mum doesn't understand how strongly you feel about Star Makers, why don't you try talking to your dad about it?"

"He doesn't understand either," I said. "He hardly ever sticks up for me when Mum's having a go. It's like he's scared of her or something."

"Oh, I'm sure he understands much more than you realize. You'd be surprised. He had dreams too, you know."

"What do you mean? Dad never talks about the past. He always says there's no point dwelling on what might have been."

Aunty Mags stared off into the distance as if she was remembering something. "Let's just say that when Crystal came along your mum and dad had to grow up pretty quickly. Your mum was all set to go off to university, but she had to turn down her place. She was brilliant you know – top of her class in everything.

I guess that's why she's always been so keen for you and Crystal to concentrate on your education. She doesn't want you to miss out – or to ever feel that way yourselves."

"Yes, but what about Dad?" I said.

"Well, your dad's always felt terrible about your mum giving up her place at uni – for some reason he blamed himself – but he had to give up some pretty important plans of his own."

I took Riley from Aunty Mags and cuddled him close. "What sort of plans? What do you mean?"

"You ask him one day," she said, tapping her nose. "You ask him about Stevie and the Stingrays."

I snorted into Riley. "Stevie and the *what*?"

"Just ask him, okay?"

I wanted to tell Aunty Mags about the wedding, ask her what she thought I should do, but I knew Crystal would kill me. Somehow, over the next few weeks, I had to get Mum to say sorry to Crystal – but I didn't even know what she was supposed to be saying sorry for.

"I'd better be getting back," I said after a bit. "Can we walk Riley again tomorrow?"

"Definitely," said Aunty Mags. "I'm going to hang around here for a bit longer but I'll call for you in the morning. And try not to get too down about Ellie. I'm sure you'll be friends again in no time."

I ran across the grass feeling so much better. I was going to talk to Dad first chance I got and I was determined to sort things out with Ellie, no matter how hard she tried to push me away. I was almost at the park exit when I noticed someone sitting on the swings. Someone with a blue baseball cap pulled right down over his eyes. It was Eddie, and he had a girl perched on his lap.

I walked a bit closer, slipping behind a tree so he wouldn't see me. He said something and the girl looked up at him laughing.

She had dark hair like Ellie.
And she was pretty like Ellie.
She even laughed a bit like Ellie.
But she wasn't Ellie.

12
The Truth About Arthur

I stumbled home in shock. My head felt as if it was about to explode with secrets, but at least everything was going to come out into the open at last. Well, everything about Eddie anyway. He was a nasty two-timing cheat and the sooner Ellie found out the better. I forgot all about Stevie and the Stingrays and asking Dad about his past. All I could think about was proving to Ellie that I'd been right about Eddie all along.

When Aunty Mags called for me in the morning I said I had too much homework to walk Riley with her. I spent most of the day rehearsing what I was going to say to Ellie. I went over it so many times it was like learning my lines for a play. Mum thought I was busy doing my homework but I was actually pacing around my room having one imaginary conversation with Ellie after another.

I couldn't wait to get to school on Monday. I knew it would be awful telling her, but I just wanted to get it over with. I hung about outside the gates for ages scanning the crowds, ready to say my piece, but there was no sign of her. When the bell rang I traipsed inside, just in time to hear the secretary give our form teacher, Mr. Bayliss, a message that Ellie had flu and was going to be off all week. I couldn't believe it. How was I supposed to keep a secret as big as this for a *whole week*? It was bad enough keeping quiet about Crystal's wedding, but this was even worse.

I was so tempted to tell Phoebe and Polly just to see what they thought – but I knew I should speak to Ellie first. I did my best to stay out of their way as much as I could just in case I blurted it out by mistake, but it was practically impossible. I spent the entire week ducking behind doors and disappearing into classrooms whenever I saw one of them coming. I felt like I was in the middle of some awful spy movie. On Thursday I was in the canteen getting my lunch when Polly called me over to sit with them.

"What's going on, Sam? You haven't been avoiding us, have you?" she said, budging up to make room for me.

"Of course not," I fibbed. "I'm just trying to learn my lines before Saturday. I've got loads you know."

"We'll test you if you want," said Phoebe.

I backed away, pulling my script out of my bag. "It's okay, thanks. I'm way better at learning stuff by myself. I've always been like that." I tried to say it lightly like it was no big deal but I could see they were hurt. "When's Ellie coming back, by the way? Do you know?"

Polly shook her head. "We're not sure – she's

really ill, you know. Maybe you should call her? Sort things out before you push *all* your friends away."

I walked off with my head in my script so they couldn't see how upset I was. I wasn't trying to push *anyone* away, but I just didn't see how I was supposed to sit there chatting away about other stuff when I had this big secret to tell about Eddie. It was easier to just keep to myself until Ellie knew the terrible truth.

I was half-hoping she wouldn't be back at drama on Saturday but I spotted her the second I walked in. She was standing right in the middle of the hall with Phoebe, Monty B and Adam and they were all laughing about something. I cleared my throat in a really exaggerated way to get her attention but when she turned round and saw it was me she turned straight back to the others and laughed even louder.

I went over to the stage to take off my jacket. The hall was boiling hot for some reason, as if someone had turned up the heating to its highest setting.

"Hi, Sam. How are you getting on with your lines?" said Mandy, coming over.

I dragged my eyes away from Ellie. "Pretty good, thanks. I know all of Act One already."

Mandy grinned. "That's brilliant, I knew I could rely on you. Listen, you couldn't do me a quick favour could you? The heating seems to be on very high and it's far too warm in here. Could you just pop along to Arthur's office and ask him to turn it down."

It was obvious she was trying to avoid Arthur, but I didn't mind – I was pleased for an excuse to get out. I wandered down the corridor, thinking about Ellie and how I was going to break the news. I kept telling myself she'd thank me in the end, but now that I'd actually seen her I wasn't so sure. Arthur's office is tucked around the corner by the toilets. I was just about to knock and go in when I heard him talking to Mrs. Beagle from the church fund-raising committee – or at least that's what I thought at first.

"*Mrs. Beagle,*" he was saying, "*we've worked together for all these years but recently...* No, no, that's no good... Let me see... *Mrs. Beagle, ever since your poor husband passed away...* Oh dear, that's not right either... *My dear Mrs. Beagle, or may I call you June? Ever since you came here to help raise money for the church, my feelings for you have deepened...*"

I put my hand up to my mouth to stop myself laughing. Mrs. Beagle wasn't in there at all. It was Arthur talking to himself and we'd obviously made a massive mistake. The love letter we found must have been for Mrs. Beagle, not Mandy, and it sounded as if he was planning to propose to her at any second. The hilarious thing was Mandy thought Arthur was in love with *her*, when he was actually madly in love with Mrs. Beagle!

I waited until I was sure I wasn't going to laugh and then I knocked on the door.

"Yes?" said Arthur, peering out.

I explained about the heating and he promised to turn it down.

"I don't know where my head is at the moment," he sighed. "I actually put the kettle in the fridge and tried to boil the milk this morning. I suppose it must be my age."

But it wasn't his age of course. It was *hormones*! And I knew all about that!

Back in the hall, Mandy had everyone round the piano.

"I'm so excited," she was saying, "because my boyfriend Julian has agreed to compose some spooky music for the show. It's going to play out all through the opening number and then whenever the phantom face appears at the window."

"Can't he compose some special music for me?" said Monty B. "Like some really cool detective music or something?"

"Sorry for being thick, yeah," said Neesha, "but what exactly *is* detective music?"

"What I'd like you to do," said Mandy, ignoring them, "is to sing the opening number in a really creepy way. Try to put across to the audience that you can't trust anyone, not even the people you think you know really well."

I looked over at Ellie. She trusted Eddie but he was a liar and a cheat and it was up to me to save her. I didn't take my eyes off her all the way through the song and whenever we sang the line *"The question of trust is one that you must be sure of – or you'll be in trouble!"* I practically yelled the words right in her face, drowning out the rest of the group.

"Calm down a bit, Sam," said Mandy. "You should be half-whispering, remember, not shouting at the top of your voice. It's great that you're so enthusiastic, but you need to listen to the others – not sing over them."

"I was just trying to get across how easy it is to trust someone when you don't really know anything about them," I said, still staring straight at Ellie.

"I swear my mum doesn't trust anyone," said Neesha. "She's totally paranoid about me speaking to strangers or answering the door or even stepping foot outside the house without her watching my every move."

"My mum's the total opposite," said Monty B. "She says *a stranger is just a friend you haven't met yet.*"

Neesha rolled her eyes. "Yeah, well no one's as strange as you, so that probably makes her feel quite safe."

"That's actually a really famous saying," said Tara, joining in, "about a stranger being a friend you haven't met. It was written by someone called Will Rodgers."

"I know another famous saying about friends," said Adam, winking at Tara. "True friends are like bras...close to your heart and always there for support." He looked over at Sandeep and they both collapsed laughing.

I stared down at the floor so no one would see my face burn up. I was actually wearing a new bra today – the most grown-up one I'd ever bought. I could just about cope with standing in the same room as Adam, but not if he was going to talk about *bras*!

"How on earth did we get on to this nonsense in the first place?" said Mandy. Sara shot her hand in the air as if Mandy was asking a real question.

"Well, Sam was singing really loud and then she said something about trusting people and Neesha said something about her mum and Monty B said something about his mum and then Neesha said something about Monty B being strange. And then Adam said something about bras."

"Thank you, Sara," said Mandy, sighing.

"Can we just get back to the song now, *please*."

"What's going on?" whispered Phoebe. "Why were you singing like that?"

"Can't say," I said. "I've got to speak to Ellie first."

Just then the door swung open and Arthur came in to check the heating was okay.

"So sorry about this morning," he said. "Silly mistake. Turned the dial up far too high."

"Not to worry," said Mandy, getting flustered. She picked up one of her music books and made out there was something terribly interesting that she just had to look at.

"The problem is," Arthur went on. "I've got something on my mind and I really would like to discuss it with you, Mandy my dear."

Mandy peeped over the top of the book. "We will discuss it, Arthur," she squeaked. "Just not right now in front of the children. Okay?"

"Splendid," he said. "Catch up with you later

then." He gave her a silly little wave and practically skipped out of the hall.

Another secret to keep, but this one was hilarious. I really *had* to tell the others but not until I'd sorted things out with Ellie. She did her level best to stay out of my way for the entire session but I finally managed to grab her just before she left to meet Eddie downstairs. I knew he was coming because she'd been harping on about it to the others all through break.

"Erm, Ellie...there's something I need to ask you," I said, as she gathered up her stuff to go.

She turned round, waiting. I was sweating like mad even though Arthur had turned the heating down.

"I was just wondering...erm...where you went with Eddie last Saturday after drama?"

Ellie looked at me suspiciously. "I didn't see him last Saturday, not that it's any of your business."

"Busy was he?" I said, fixing her with my Most Meaningful Stare.

"What are you getting at, Sam? I didn't see him because it was his nephew's first birthday. Happy?"

She pushed past me and ran downstairs.

I ran down after her but she was through the doors before I could catch up. "He wasn't with his nephew," I shouted. "He's a liar!" But I have no idea if she heard. I trailed back up to get my things and by the time I got back down and out of the building they were already halfway up the High Road, a whole crowd of them with Eddie and Ellie right in the middle.

I set off after them, determined to catch up. I was still going to tell her about what he was up to, whether she wanted to hear it or not. That's what friends are supposed to do, isn't it?

13
A Question of Trust

I was charging up the High Road ready to confront Eddie when Crystal rang.

"Hey, Sam, what are you up to?"

"Oh you know, just stalking my ex-best friend to save her from her evil two-timing boyfriend," I said. It sounded so stupid I started to giggle.

"Look, don't go after them now, come and meet me instead. I've just found the most amazing dress for you to wear at the wedding. It's got this sort of dusty-pink tutu style skirt with layers and layers of lace, and I really want you to try it on."

I glanced up as Ellie and Eddie disappeared round the corner. I really wanted to sort things out, but it would have to wait until Monday. Crystal gave me directions to the shop, a little retro-boutique not that far from where I was.

The dress was much more Crystal's style than mine but there was no telling her and in the end I agreed to try it on just to shut her up.

"Oh, look at you," she cried, pulling me out of the changing room and twirling me round in front of the mirror. "My little sister, all grown up!"

The dress was stiff and uncomfortable. I wriggled about while Crystal went on and on about the colour and length and how she was going to go straight back to her flat and make me a matching crystal necklace. "I'll just get changed," I said in the end. The lace was itching my legs and I couldn't wait to get it off.

Walking back from the shop with the new dress in a bag, I told Crystal about Eddie and seeing him in the park with another girl. "I wanted to warn Ellie after drama, I did try, but she ran off before I could explain properly."

Crystal shook her head. "Listen, Sam, I know it sounds harsh but if I was you I'd let Ellie find out for herself. She probably won't even believe you anyway – she'll think you're just saying it to be spiteful. I know you're just trying to be a good friend, but she won't thank you for it."

"Yeah, but how am I supposed to *not* tell her? It's like your wedding."

Crystal looked at me sharply. "What do you mean? What has Ellie's low-life boyfriend got to do with *my* wedding?"

"Just that I really want to tell Mum and Dad. I'm serious, Crystal, I can't carry on pretending that everything's normal when you're about to get married and they don't have the first clue."

I still hadn't told Crystal about Sophia Malone's wedding and Mum doing the flowers.

I knew I should, but I was scared it might make everything worse.

"I am going to tell them," Crystal said quietly.

"But Crystal, there's not that much time left and what if they find out before you tell them? They'll be so hurt."

Crystal rounded on me. "But what about *me* being hurt? I don't want Mum spoiling the most important day of my life! She can't even bring herself to say Tyler's name, so she's not exactly going to welcome him into the family."

"But what about Dad?" I could feel myself getting really angry. It was crazy. Crystal and Dad had always been so close. She couldn't get married without telling him! It would break his heart.

She scuffed her boots along the ground. "I don't want to talk about it any more. You don't understand. Anyway I've got to get back now. I've got work to do." She sloped off in a mood.

I felt like running after her to say sorry but I didn't really know what I'd be saying sorry for.

I skulked home with the dress. Mum was at work, but I had to sneak past Dad. He was in the living room, singing along to some old CD, but I don't think he even noticed I was home.

I didn't see Crystal at all the following week. I called her a few times but she said she was too busy making jewellery or sorting things out for the wedding to meet up. I kept on at her to tell Mum and Dad she was getting married, but she wouldn't budge. It was a total nightmare. I had the stiff, itchy dress stuffed at the back of my wardrobe and the invitation to the wedding hidden under my mattress – but I knew there was no way on earth that I'd be able to go without telling Mum and Dad first. And what about Sophia Malone and helping out at *her* wedding? I couldn't exactly cut myself in half.

Nothing had changed much with Ellie either. We still weren't talking and she was still hanging out with Eddie and his mates. Sometimes I'd catch her looking at me during a lesson or at lunchtime, and a couple of times I nearly went over to try and patch things up – but after what Crystal said about Ellie not believing me, I couldn't quite bring myself to do it.

Phoebe and Polly were desperate to help. They kept coming up with new ways of getting us back together, but it was hopeless. I never realized Ellie could be so stubborn – or maybe Eddie was just filling her head with terrible lies, even though he didn't actually know the first thing about me.

"Why don't we ask her to come to the school fireworks next week?" Phoebe suggested the next Saturday during break at drama. "It might be different if we weren't at school or Star Makers. She might kind of forget she was angry with you…" I looked across at Ellie. She was on the other side of the hall with Neesha, even though Polly had asked them to sit with us. I shook my head. "It wouldn't make the slightest difference. She wouldn't care if we were in Outer Mongolia, she still wouldn't talk to me."

"Well there must be *something* we can do." Phoebe sighed. "You haven't been yourself at all since the row."

"What, you mean she's been so much nicer!" said Monty B, munching his way through a *second* packet of cheese-and-onion crisps.

"Who asked you?" I snapped.

"Phew, that's better," he said. "Back to normal. Anyway, if you really want to turn Ellie against Eddie, why don't you tell her that he's a crazed axe-murderer and he's just been released from prison?"

"I actually know something about Eddie already," I said, leaning in to whisper. "But I can't say what it is and I'm not going to tell Ellie either."

They all stopped eating and stared at me.

"Come on, Sam," breathed Phoebe. "What do you know?"

"He's not married is he?" said Monty B.

"*Married?*" I spluttered, nearly choking on my drink. "He's fourteen years old!"

"What is it then? And how did you find out?"

"You haven't been stalking them have you?" said Polly.

I almost laughed. "Of course not, but I can't tell you because I have to tell Ellie first, and I can't tell Ellie because she won't believe me."

"Well, why don't you tell *me* and I'll tell *her*?" said Monty B. "I won't even mention your name."

"What are you lot up to?" said Mandy, coming over. "You look like you're cooking up some evil plan, the way you're huddled up with your heads together!"

"We're just discussing the show," said Monty B. "It's nothing sinister, Mandy. Trust me."

"It's funny you should say that because we're going to be doing some *trust* games straight after break."

"What do you mean?" I said, my heart missing a beat. "Not those awful ones where you have to fall into people's arms and stuff?"

"Yes, something like that," said Mandy. "But don't look so worried, Sam. Trust games are really important for building a sense of closeness and support in the group. I know *The Phantom Face* is about a group of people who don't trust each other, but if you guys don't feel really close when you're performing, the show won't be nearly as good as I know it could be." She looked right at me. "*Trust me*, Sam! It'll be fun."

Oh yes, it would be great fun! Closing my eyes and falling back into Adam's arms – or even worse, Ellie's! The way things were going at the moment, she'd probably drop me straight onto the floor.

The first game was bad enough. It was called Blindfold Find and basically we had to stand in a space in the hall with our eyes closed while Mandy called out a load of instructions, like, "Find someone with the same length hair as you," or, "Find someone with a nose like yours." Everyone was in hysterics as they stumbled about, running their hands through people's hair or grabbing hold of their noses to see what shape they were. At one point someone came over and placed a hand on my head. I knew it was Ellie straight away; I could just tell. I opened my eyes a tiny bit to peek and she opened hers at the same time. "No cheating!" Mandy called from the front. "Keep your eyes closed tight!"

"Talking of cheating," I nearly said to Ellie, but she'd moved away and it was too late.

The second game was called Still Pond and

it was even worse. One person was blindfolded while everyone else moved around the room, and then when Mandy called out "Still Pond" we had to freeze. The blindfolded person then had to feel around for someone and try to guess who they were by touching them.

Neesha was first to be blindfolded. When Mandy called out "Still Pond" she shuffled over to Monty B and then said his name without laying a hand on him.

"Hey! How did you know it was me?" he said.

"Oh my God, yeah, from your cheese-and-onion breath! It's minging! Ever heard of sucking on a mint?"

"Oh, that's charming," said Monty B. "You don't smell so great yourself!"

Mandy was trying not to laugh. "Come on, guys, we're supposed to be bonding, not hurling insults at each other."

Adam asked to go next. As soon as he was

blindfolded I darted off to the furthest end of the hall, desperate to stay out of his way – but it was like we were both wearing super-strength magnets or something. When Mandy shouted "Still Pond", he lurched straight towards me, passing at least fifteen other people on the way.

He reached out and his hand brushed my left shoulder. I stopped breathing and took a silent but massive step to my right. "Hey, where are you?" he said, waving his arms about. "Stop moving!" He found me again and had a hand on each side of my face when Arthur walked in. It was like a miracle. I never thought I'd be so pleased to see him!

"Oh, this looks like fun, Mandy," he boomed. "Perhaps I could have a turn?"

"Erm...perhaps not," said Mandy. "We're just about to go onto the next game, you see." She whipped the blindfold off Adam. "Come and make a circle everyone."

We wandered into the middle to make a

circle while Mandy chatted to Arthur. It was something quite boring about locking up at the end of the session, but she was obviously dead scared he was going to declare his undying love for her every time he made an appearance.

When we went downstairs at the end of the session, Eddie was waiting for Ellie, his cap pulled down even further over his eyes than usual. It was weird but he barely said hello or even looked at her as they sloped out of the car park together. Ellie didn't look happy at all but she went off with him anyway.

I had planned to go back to Phoebe's for the afternoon and practise some scenes, but Crystal was waiting for me on the other side of the road. She was hopping from foot to foot, and I could see she was totally hyped up about something. It was so typical of her to disappear for days on end and then turn up like this, out of the blue.

"Remember I said Tyler and the Garlic Pickers were waiting for some BIG news," she said, practically dragging me off down the road. "Well, they're meeting with their agent right now, like this second, and Tyler's going to text me as soon as he knows. It's the big break they've been waiting for, I'm sure of it."

We wandered down to the park and sat in our usual place on the swings. I told her about drama and how Ellie was still ignoring me, but I could tell she wasn't really listening.

"Earth to Crystal," I said, waving my hand in front of her face.

"Sorry, Sam," she said. "I can't stop thinking about the meeting. Tyler's going to ring me any minute."

"But what about the wedding? When are you going to tell Mum and Dad?" I knew she was sick of hearing it but I couldn't help myself. I was so *sick* of keeping it a secret. Crystal fiddled around with her phone, staring at the screen as if she could somehow force it to ring.

"Look, Crystal – if you don't tell Mum and Dad about the wedding then I'm not coming either."

Crystal didn't say anything for a long time.

"I don't care," she said in the end. Her voice was shaking. "Tyler's my family now."

"Don't say that!" I gasped, grabbing her swing. "I know you don't mean that. *I'm* your family, and Mum and Dad. If you didn't care, you wouldn't be so upset. I know you're hurt, Crystal, but we all miss you so much – not just me – *all* of us."

She looked away, her eyes filling with tears.

"Look, I don't know what Mum said to you that night but if you get married without telling her it's like you're cutting her right out of your life!"

Crystal jumped off the swing. "You mean the way she wanted to cut *me* right out of hers!"

"What do you mean?"

She started to walk off, calling over her shoulder, "Why don't you ask her, Sam?" She stopped walking for a second and turned back towards me. She was crying now. Big fat tears running down her face. "If you want to know why Mum and I aren't talking, why don't you just ask her?"

Dumped!

I had every intention of asking Mum the second I got home – and this time I was determined to get an answer – but with all the drama of seeing Crystal, I'd somehow forgotten that today was the day Dad was whisking Mum off to Paris for their anniversary. I arrived home to find them both upstairs packing.

Dad was singing some song about the Mona Lisa while Mum held up one dress after the other, trying to decide what to take. "You'd better get sorted for going to Aunty Mags's," she said as I walked into their room. "Don't forget to take all your school stuff and your uniform and lots of clean knickers—"

"*Mum!* I'm not a baby!"

"I know but—"

"Rosy, stop fussing," said Dad. "I mean, talk about the Mona Lisa – it's more like the Mona *Rosa*!"

"Hey you!" Mum pretended to slap Dad and they fell back on the bed, giggling.

I left them to it. They were so excited about Paris there was no way I could start asking questions about Crystal and the night of her birthday now. I tried to convince myself that everything would be okay in the end, although it was difficult to imagine Mum and Crystal making up in time for the wedding. And even if they did, Crystal was getting married on the same day as Sophia Malone, which meant that at some point Mum was going to have to choose between her own daughter's wedding and the biggest job of her life.

I loved being at Aunty Mags's house. It was like

being on holiday myself. I didn't speak to Crystal at all and, with Mum and Dad away, I decided to try and push it all to the back of mind until they came home. It was less than a month till the wedding, but it wasn't like I could do anything about it.

On Friday night, Aunty Mags's best friend Stevie came over for a takeaway. Aunty Mags and Stevie have been best friends for years. I think they used to go out with each other, but that was way before I was born. Stevie hadn't met Riley yet, but he was totally smitten from the second he walked in.

"I don't believe it, Mags – he's just like Kasper!" he cried, scooping Riley up in his arms. Riley squirmed about, desperate to plant as many kisses on Stevie's face as he could.

"Who's Kasper?" I asked, laughing at Riley.

"*What?*" Aunty Mags looked at me, shocked. "Kasper was your dad's dog, Sam, he *must've* told you. He got him for his tenth birthday.

They were totally inseparable for years."

"He's never mentioned it," I said. "Mum's a real cat person so we've never even talked about getting a dog."

"I'll dig out some old photos later," said Aunty Mags. "I'm sure I've got some upstairs."

It was such a funny evening, the best I'd had in ages. Stevie had me in stitches, telling me stories about Aunty Mags and Dad when they were teenagers. "I had a terrible crush on Mags," he said, winking at Aunty Mags. "That's why I used to hang around with your dad all the time."

"So you mean you were Dad's friend first?"

"That's right," said Stevie, "but like I said, I only used to come over so I could see Mags."

Aunty Mags laughed. "It was Kasper you loved. You used to take him out for walks and pretend he was *your* dog, remember?"

"I remember him getting hold of my new drumsticks. He chewed them to pieces!"

"Riley's a horror for chewing as well," moaned Aunty Mags. "I mean look at the state of this room…"

She stopped talking suddenly and leaped up as Riley came bounding through the door with my new bra trailing out of his mouth. "Oh no!" I shouted, leaping up as well.

"Riley Lester!" said Stevie in a very stern voice. "Drop!"

Riley looked up at Stevie with his huge brown eyes and for a second I thought he was going to obey, but just then the takeaway arrived and he bounded out again, my new, half-chewed bra flying out behind him.

Later on that night I was in bed reading when Aunty Mags came in with some old photos of Kasper. Stevie was right – he looked exactly like Riley, only much bigger.

"I found something else at the back of the cupboard," said Aunty Mags. "I haven't looked at this for a while." She handed me an ancient scrapbook stuffed full of newspaper cuttings. "Remember when we talked in the park that time? Well, he'll probably kill me for showing you, but I think you should know what your old dad used to get up to." She gave me a kiss and left me to it.

The newspaper cuttings were all about a local band called Stevie and the Stingrays. I could see straight away that Dad was in the band and so was Stevie. Dad was holding a guitar. He looked cool and trendy and very, very young. My Dad In A Band. How had he kept something as big as *that* hidden for so many years?

I pored over the cuttings, reading every word. Stevie and the Stingrays had played in pubs and clubs all over the country. They'd got rave reviews for practically all their gigs. *Stevie and the Stingrays...a band who show that they know how to craft a catchy tune... We can pin our local pride on these four lads...the vocals are crisp, the guitar is understated yet inspired...an energetic crash of noise... Stevie and the Stingrays are on the cusp of something special....a local band to be proud of...*

Most of the cuttings were from nineteen years ago. A year before Crystal was born. Dad must've dropped out of the band when Mum got pregnant. That's what Aunty Mags meant when she said Dad had to give up his dreams too. I wondered if that was the end of Stevie and the Stingrays, or if they'd found someone to replace Dad.

My head was swimming. Mum must have known Dad when he was in the band. So that meant she fell in love with a musician, just like Crystal! How could one family have so many secrets? I closed the scrapbook and lay back on my bed, staring at the ceiling. As soon as Mum and Dad got back I was going to tell them *everything*, and I wanted a whole load of answers from them as well.

* * *

When I got to drama on Saturday, Julian was in the car park with Mandy, unloading some equipment from his van. Polly arrived at the same time and we helped them carry everything upstairs.

"Goodness me. What's all this?" said Arthur, peering out of his office as we hauled everything up.

"Oh hello, Arthur. You know my *boyfriend* Julian, don't you?" said Mandy, emphasizing the word "boyfriend" just to make sure he got the message. Mandy actually met Julian through Arthur when he turned up to build the set for one of Arthur's plays on the same day as *our* dress rehearsal!

"Yes of course!" boomed Arthur, tugging at his beard. "Julian and I go way back. Do let me know if you need any help."

It took about three trips to get everything up. There was a drum set and a synthesizer and all sorts of lighting equipment.

"This looks wicked!" said Sandeep, hobbling over on his crutches.

"Great," said Mandy, "because your new role from now on is assistant stage technician. How does that sound?"

"It sounds brilliant. Something useful to do at last."

We all crowded round Julian as he set up his instruments.

"Have you composed the detective music yet?" said Monty B. "I'll need something dignified but catchy."

"What character are you playing then?" asked Julian, grinning.

"I'm Detective Biscuit," said Monty B, "but I'm not your common Jammy Dodger. I've got a bit more class than that – like a nice chocolate digestive or a—"

"*Class!*" snorted Neesha. "More like *farce* if you ask me." She made a face at Ellie and they both cracked up.

"Oh, you're funny," said Monty B and stuck his tongue out at them, blowing a raspberry.

"Thank you," said Neesha. "I rest my case."

When Julian was ready, he got us all up onstage to sing the opening number. He wanted to record us singing so he could work out where the sound effects and backing music needed to fit in. He'd also set up a special screen called a shark-tooth scrim, and every time Adam and I saw the phantom face at the window, he was going to project this really creepy image of an old-fashioned looking girl in a long white nightie.

"Oh, she looks just like you, Phoebe!" cried Sara, when Julian showed us the image. "You know, in your white nightie with the pretty ruffles round the collar."

"Shut up!" hissed Phoebe.

"Okay! Keep your frilly knickers on," said Sara, and Phoebe slapped her across the head.

"Phoebe! What are you doing?" said Mandy, shocked. "I thought things had calmed down since our session of trust games."

"Don't worry," said Monty B. "I'll keep her under control. It's her temper, you see."

Phoebe raised her hand to hit him as well and then dropped it again, sighing.

We went over and over the opening number while Julian played around with the sound effects. Finally, when he was happy, Mandy sent us off to have a break.

"Hey, Sam, we found a home for the last of the puppies yesterday," Adam said, taking a sandwich out of his bag. We were all sitting together in a big group and so far I'd managed to avoid any direct eye contact with him. Keep A Low Profile...that was my latest coping strategy. It was obvious he fancied Catharine, but that didn't stop me acting like an idiot every time I was anywhere near him. "Mum's quite relieved in a way," he went on. "They're terrible chewers, you know. They'd destroyed three of my exercise books already!"

"Oh, Riley's a terrible chewer as well," I said, forgetting my strategy in the blink of an eye. "You should have seen him last night when he got hold of my new bra..." The word was out of my mouth before I knew what I was saying. "I mean my new braaaaaaaaaaa..." I repeated, stretching the last sound out while I desperately tried to think of something else to say. "My new braaaaaaaan jumper. Hahaha!"

Adam looked at me as if I was deranged. "What do you mean, your new *braaaaaaaaan* jumper?"

Everyone stopped what they were doing and looked at us.

"I know what she means," said Monty B. "I've got a braaaaaaaaan jumper myself. My nan knitted it for me. It's a kind of cross between your ordinary brown and a sort of green army colour."

"What?" said Adam.

"I thought I had the only one actually. It's not exactly the coolest colour combination in the world, is it, Sam?"

I snorted into my script. I didn't have a clue what Monty B was on about but I could've literally kissed him for coming to my rescue.

Back at Aunty Mags's I sat on the couch cuddling Riley, thinking about Stevie and the Stingrays and how weird it was to find out something so crazy about my own dad.

"Are you okay, love?" said Aunty Mags, coming in with a pot of tea and some biscuits. "It's your school fireworks tonight, isn't it? I could drop you up there if you want."

I shook my head. "I'm not going. I'm not in the mood."

Aunty Mags sat down next to me on the

couch. "How was drama today? Is the show going well?"

I nodded, cuddling in to Aunty Mags and helping myself to a biscuit. "It was brilliant. Mandy's boyfriend Julian was there, sorting out the music and sound effects. It's going to be such a great show. I just wish my mum would realize how serious I am about acting. She carries on and on as if being on the stage would be a fate worse than death – and now I find out that my boring old dad, who works in a boring old bank, was in a *band*. It just doesn't make sense. I know he's always humming and tapping his feet and singing random songs from the past, but that's not the same as being in a band. Why do you think he's never told me?"

Aunty Mags shrugged. "I don't know, darling, he doesn't really talk about it any more, but I guess it explains where you get your love of performing from, eh?"

"I suppose so, but I still don't get it. I mean

why did he leave Stevie and the Stingrays if they were doing so well?"

"It was because of the baby, Sam. You see, when your dad found out your mum was expecting Crystal, he knew he couldn't carry on with the band. They were travelling all over the place, playing at a different venue every night of the week. He didn't want to put your mum through that. He was good though – really good – but your mum always came first. They met at a gig, you know."

"No way! But Mum's so serious about everything. I always thought she fell in love with Dad when he was already working at the bank."

"Nope, she met him before that. She was only eighteen, all set to go off to uni, when she went to see Stevie and the Stingrays. Your dad says he spotted her the second he walked out onstage. He says it was as if everyone else in the crowd just disappeared."

"But whenever I've asked my mum where she met my dad, she's always said it was through an old friend."

Aunty Mags grinned. "Well, that's because your mum was at the gig with *me*."

"You mean *you* were the friend?" My mouth fell open. It was all falling into place. "What about the band? What happened to Stevie and the others when Dad left?"

"They never really recovered, to tell you the truth. They tried out a few new guitarists, but none of them worked out."

"But if Mum fell in love with Dad when he was in a band, why is she so dead set against Crystal going out with Tyler?"

Aunty Mags put her arm round me and pulled me close for a cuddle, Riley squashed between us in the middle. "She's just worried, Sam. She just doesn't want Crystal to make the same mistakes she made – not that meeting your dad was a mistake – but she was so young and..."

"Well, the thing is," I said, suddenly desperate to tell her about the wedding.

"The thing is what?" she said.

And then my phone rang.

And it was Ellie.

And she was crying.

"I've been dumped!" she sobbed down the phone. "Eddie has just dumped me with a *TEXT*! Can you come over right now, Sam... *Please!*"

15
Friends First!

I gave Aunty Mags a hug, told her I had to go – and left before she could ask any questions. Crystal's wedding and all of that would have to wait. I literally ran all the way over to Ellie's. I didn't care about the row or anything, I just wanted to see her. She was still crying when she opened the door.

"Can you believe it?" she sobbed, dragging me in. "A *text!*"

"What happened? What did he say?"

She opened her phone and held it up to show me:

2 busy revising 2 c u...lets cool things...btw can I have my grey hoodie back?

"I know he's got exams coming up but he

kept saying he wasn't bothered, that revising was for idiots."

"He's the idiot! And what a cheek – asking for his grey hoodie back!"

"But that's the worst thing," she spluttered. "You won't believe it, Sam, but I've only gone and..."

"...lost it?" I finished for her. "Oh Ellie, trust you." I gave her a look and she half-grinned at me through her tears and suddenly we were laughing and laughing until we were bent over, clutching hold of the banister.

"It's not funny," she moaned. "I've been so stupid..."

"He's the one who's stupid," I said. "*All* boys are stupid."

I decided right that second not to tell her about the girl in the park. There didn't seem to be any point.

"Hey, let's go upstairs," she said, pulling my arm. "I don't want my mum to know. She'd been nagging me to stop seeing Eddie for ages. Ever since I met him."

It was weird being back in Ellie's room. I sat on the edge of the bed, not sure if everything was okay between us or not.

"I meant it, you know," she said, sitting down next to me. "I have been stupid. My mum warned me and you warned me but I was too stubborn to listen and you don't know what it's been like. He kept telling me who to talk to and who to be friends with and everything."

"But why didn't you just tell him to get lost?"

Ellie shrugged. "It was just so exciting when we met at the disco on holiday. And then I kept hoping it could be like that again, but it wasn't. He just wanted to hang out with his friends and it was so boring and he kept saying horrible things about you all the time."

"What a creep!" I said.

"I know, and remember what I always used to say? Friends First..."

"Yeah, but it's my fault as well. I kept going on and on at you and...I was a tiny bit jealous, if you want to know the truth." I blushed a bit. "I just thought that, you know, I'd be the first one to have a boyfriend."

"But he wasn't even my boyfriend. Not really. Anyway, what about you and Adam? He asked you back to his house that day after drama, didn't he?"

"He did, but then when I turned up he was out with *Catharine*! I don't know if they're actually going out, but he obviously wasn't bothered about waiting in to see me. I felt like a right lemon."

"No, he's the lemon," said Ellie. "Eddie's an idiot and Adam's a lemon and we don't need either of them!"

We had a brilliant afternoon. It was just like old times. We talked and talked and listened to music and tried out some of the dances we'd learned for the show. When Aunty Mags called to see what time I was coming home, Ellie begged me to stay.

"Come on, Sam, *please*. We haven't had a sleepover for ages."

It was supposed to be my last night at Aunty Mags's – Mum and Dad weren't due back till gone midnight – but she said it was fine and that I should just pop over to pick up my stuff before it got too late.

We decided to go back together. We ran down the road, holding hands in the dark.

"You realize we're missing the school fireworks tonight," I said, as a rocket exploded above us and hundreds of tiny stars sprayed out across the sky.

"I'm so not in the mood," said Ellie. "How about you?"

I smiled, shaking my head. "That's exactly what I said to Aunty Mags just before you rang."

When we got there, Ellie played with Riley

while I went upstairs to pack my things. I had one last look at the scrapbook and then left it on my bed for Aunty Mags.

"It's nice to see you two are friends again," said Aunty Mags when I came down. "Life's too short to fight."

I gave her the biggest hug, squeezing as tight as I could. "Thanks for a brilliant week and thanks for telling me about Dad," I whispered. "Maybe we can find some way to get Stevie and the Stingrays back together…"

She hugged me back, laughing. "Have a lovely time. And listen, if you *really* want to be an actress, if you're *that* serious about it…"

"I *am*, Aunty Mags. I want it more than anything."

"Well, then you'll make it happen, sweetheart. I know you will."

Back at Ellie's we sat about in our pyjamas, watching the first two Star Maker shows on DVD, even though we'd already seen them about a million times before. Our favourite bit out of both shows is when Monty B dresses up as a Christmas fairy in this hilarious song called "*Scream!*"

"And Eddie kept saying drama was for losers!" joked Ellie, as Monty B pranced about the stage in his pink tutu. We played it over and over, leaping around the room pretending to be Monty B and screaming at the tops of our voices, until Ellie's mum came in to see what was going on.

"Sorry," said Ellie. "We didn't realize we were being so noisy. Hey, you haven't seen my grey hoodie, have you, Mum? Like, in the wash or something? Only I can't find it anywhere."

Ellie's mum rolled her eyes and we started to giggle. "What are you two like?" she said, and in a funny sort of way it was as if the last two months had never happened.

I waited until the lights were out and we were snuggled under the covers before I told

Ellie about Crystal. Ellie was in her bed and I was on one of those blow-up mattresses next to her. I couldn't see her face, but every now and then she whispered "No way", and "You're joking", and "I don't believe it".

"It's such a relief to talk about it," I said after a bit, hugging my pillow and trying not to cry.

"And your mum's got no idea?"

I stared up into the darkness. "No, she doesn't know about them getting married or that it's on the same day as Sophia Malone's wedding. Something happened between my mum and Crystal on the night of Crystal's eighteenth birthday. Crystal told Mum that she was giving up her place at uni and it sparked off this massive row and my mum said something and now Crystal's waiting for her to say sorry. The thing is, my mum's in such a state about Crystal living with Tyler and giving up her place at uni that I don't think she even realizes how hurt Crystal is."

"So what *did* your mum say to Crystal that night?"

"I don't know. That's what's so frustrating. No one will tell me. And that's not all – I just found out yesterday that my dad used to be in a band."

"Whoa! You're really starting to worry me now, Sam! *Your* dad, *in a band?*"

"I know it sounds crazy, but I've seen the newspaper cuttings. It's true, Ellie. He used to play guitar in a band called Stevie and the Stingrays. They were really big, like twenty years ago."

"But *your dad?*" said Ellie weakly.

"I know; I can't believe it either. Anyway, all this stuff's been happening, and I've been trying to work out what to do about Crystal and Mum, but it's all such a mess and I haven't been able to tell anyone..."

The words hung in the dark between us.

"I mean, you know, because it was a secret..."

"No it's okay," said Ellie quietly. She climbed into my bed and cuddled up close. "I know I've been a terrible friend. I don't know what was wrong with me. Eddie said all these awful things about you and I just believed him. It's like he reprogrammed my brain or something. I am *never* going to put a boy in front of my friends again."

"He didn't reprogram your brain, Ellie," I said, giggling. "It's called hormones. Oh, and talking of hormones, that reminds me. Arthur isn't interested in Mandy at all – it's Mrs. Beagle he's in love with."

"No way!" Ellie snorted. *"Mrs. Beagle?"*

"I know, it's hilarious, isn't it?"

"Oh, my darling Mrs. Beagle! I cannot keep my feelings trapped inside me for one moment longer!" Ellie squealed, throwing the covers off and leaping on top of me.

"Oi, get off!" I shrieked, pushing her away.

We sat up, out of breath and laughing.

"Seriously though, Sam," said Ellie, when she'd got her breath back, "this stuff about Crystal and her wedding... You have *got* to tell your mum. Like, straight away. Imagine if Crystal went ahead with the wedding and then your mum found out that you'd known about it all along."

I knew Ellie was right. It was only three weeks until the wedding and no matter how angry Mum was with Crystal, it would break her heart for ever if Crystal got married without telling her – and even though Crystal would never admit it, I think it would break her heart as well. She might say that Tyler was her family now, but I bet if she got married without Mum knowing she'd end up regretting it for the rest of her life.

I walked home the next morning after breakfast determined to tell Mum and Dad everything. I wasn't exactly looking forward to it. When Mum found out about the wedding she'd probably go off like the biggest firework of all time – I could literally imagine her pinging off the walls – but it had to be done. I let myself in and stood for a second in the hall.

"*Bonjour!*" I called out. "Is anyone here?"

"Sam?"

It was Mum. I looked up. She was standing at the top of the stairs, clutching something in her hand.

"What's the matter?" I said.

She didn't say anything. She just stood there, frozen.

"What's the matter?" I said again. "Why are you standing there like that? You're freaking me out…"

"What's this?" she said in the end.

I couldn't *see* what it was, she was too far up the stairs, but suddenly I knew. My heart started to bang against my ribs.

It was the invitation to Crystal's wedding.

16

On or Off?

I raced up the stairs three at a time and snatched the invitation out of Mum's hand. I felt like I'd betrayed Crystal *and* Mum all at the same time.

"I was going to tell you today, I swear. I know you won't believe me but it's true – you can ask Ellie…"

"I don't understand," said Mum. Big tears started to roll down her face. "Crystal can't be getting married. She's only known Tyler for five minutes. You don't get married when you're eighteen…"

I pulled a tissue out of my pocket. "Mum, stop crying. You've just got to sort things out. I mean, *you* got married young, didn't you?"

"*Dave!*" Mum shouted out to Dad.

"Hang on," he called back, "I'm on the phone."

She sank down onto the top stair. "I know why she's doing this," she said weakly. "It's to punish me. It's not because she loves Tyler or anything. She's only doing it because she knows it's the one thing that would—"

"No, she really loves Tyler," I interrupted. "You should see how she talks about him. How proud she is. He's about to get a recording contract and everything..."

Mum snorted into her tissue. "Do me a favour..."

"What's going on?" said Dad, coming out of their bedroom.

Mum took the invitation out of my hand and held it up to him. The tears started to run down her face again.

"Do something, Dave. Go and talk to her – she won't listen to me. Go round there and bring her home, *please*."

Dad was staring at the invitation, his mouth tight.

"I knew something like this would happen," he said, getting angry. "I can't just go round there and drag her back. I told you to sort things out months ago, Rosy. Why have you let things get *so* out of hand?"

Mum jumped up and pulled his arm. She was desperate. "I did try and sort it out. I called and called but she wouldn't speak to me or see me. Just go round there," she sobbed. "Go round there and say we're sorry and that we want her back with us. That she can start her course next year."

Dad pulled his arm away. "No, Rosy! I'll go round there but I'm not going to start a row. Crystal needs to know we love her no matter what she decides to do with her life."

He grabbed a jacket from his room and ran downstairs. I raced down after him. "Tell her it wasn't my fault," I said. "I don't want her to think I told you. She *trusted* me."

"Why *didn't* you tell us?" Mum shouted down. "Don't you realize how serious this is?"

I trailed back up to my room and lay on my bed. I could've called Crystal to warn her Dad was on his way but I was scared she might do a runner. I wanted Dad to talk to her. I didn't care if she was mad at me afterwards – I just wanted things to go back to the way they were before.

Dad was gone for ages. It was awful, waiting. I could hear Mum pacing around, working herself up into a terrible state. After a bit, she came into my room. "How *could* you go behind my back?" she wailed, wringing her hands. "How long have you two been plotting this together? You're just as bad as her – you'll both end up throwing your lives away!"

It was awful; like she thought me and Crystal were one person and if Crystal messed up then

I was going to mess up as well. Not that Crystal *had* messed up – not in my eyes anyway.

By the time Dad got back, Mum had driven herself into a total frenzy, going on and on about opportunities and the future and how we only get one chance to make something of ourselves. I felt like shaking her and shouting *I am Sam! Sam I am!* like when I was a little girl, but I knew it wouldn't make the slightest difference. Mum had decided I was some sort of CRYSTAL CLONE and that was that.

"The wedding's off," said Dad. We were sitting round the kitchen table – desperate to hear what had happened. "It's got nothing to do with me," he went on before Mum could get a word in. "She said they'd had to postpone it for other reasons."

"Well, thank heavens for that," said Mum, her voice shaky. She reached over and put her hand over Dad's. "When's she coming home?"

"She's not coming home," said Dad. "She

doesn't even want to see us at the moment."

"But I don't understand," said Mum. Her eyes filled with tears again and Dad squeezed her hand.

"Look, Rosy, I don't understand exactly what went on between the two of you, but Crystal's very hurt and unless you go and talk to her yourself it's just going to get worse."

"But why's the wedding off? She's bought me a dress and everything," I cried, totally confused. "Mum, why can't you just go round there and say sorry? I know Crystal's eighteen and she can live where she wants, but I can't bear it any more, the way things are between you two. It's not just you who's suffering!"

Mum's shoulder's sagged.

"What is it, Rosy?" said Dad. "Sam's right. Why can't you just go round there and say sorry? You're her mother, for goodness' sake. It's up to you to sort this out."

"But don't you see?" said Mum. "If I say

sorry she'll think everything's okay. All those years of hard work, all that effort, and for what? She was the top of her class. *The brightest girl they'd ever had in the school,* one teacher said to me. And now she's selling jewellery at markets. She could be doing anything with her life. *Anything!* Don't you get it? If I go round there and say sorry, I'll *never* get her back! Never!" Mum scraped back her chair and ran out of the room.

Dad sat there with his head in his hands. "What a nightmare," he muttered. "I've always tried to do the right thing but it's all turned out to be such a mess."

I went round to give him a hug. I knew it was the wrong moment, but I was dying to ask him about the band. He looked so tired and worn out, it was difficult to imagine it was actually *him* in those newspaper cuttings. If only I could turn back time – even for a day – just to see what he was really like.

"I'll talk to Crystal," I said. "I'll try to make her understand that Mum *is* sorry – she just doesn't know how to say it."

But it looked as if Crystal wasn't talking to *me* either. Every time I called her it went straight to voicemail and she obviously had no intention of ringing me back. I didn't even know if the wedding really was off or if she'd just said that to get rid of Dad.

"I've *got* to find out what's going on." It was Monday morning and I was outside school with Ellie. "I don't know if the wedding's cancelled or when Crystal's going to call me. Mum's moping around the house like the world's about to come to an end and Crystal probably feels like she can't trust me any more anyway."

"And what about drama? Does your mum know you're Laura yet? You don't want her to stop you doing it at the last minute."

I shook my head. "She doesn't know and there's no way I could tell her – not now."

"Don't tell me you two are talking again," said Phoebe, walking over. "This is like the best news ever."

"Yeah, well Sam was right about Eddie all along," said Ellie, pulling a face. "He's history as far as I'm concerned."

"Best place for him," I said. But it was going to take a miracle to sort out everything else.

I didn't hear anything from Crystal over the next few days. She obviously thought I'd blabbed to Mum and betrayed her and that's why she wasn't returning my calls. I hated not knowing where she was or how to get in touch with her. I swore that the second I heard from her I was going to force her to tell me where she lived so at least I'd know where to find her the next time she gave me the silent treatment.

On Thursday morning I was sitting in French when Ellie burst in late. I could see straight away that something was up. She was trying to mouth something to me across the room but I couldn't make out what it was. Madame Blanc gave me a look, so I shook my head at Ellie and went back to the exercise I was doing. She was easily one of the strictest teachers in the school and getting into trouble was the last thing I needed right then if I was going to keep Mum off my back.

A few minutes later Tara Perkins passed me a note. I didn't even have time to see what it said before Madame Blanc whipped it out of my hand.

"Passing notes in class," she snapped, tearing the grubby piece of paper into tiny pieces. "Detention for both of you, after school tomorrow, my room."

"But I didn't do anything," I pleaded. Mum was going to flip if she found out I had a detention. Madame Blanc raised one eyebrow and turned away. I could get down on my knees and beg and it wouldn't make the slightest difference. She'd never backed down on a detention in her life. Ellie looked over at me, shrugging. She looked really upset. "Sorry," she mouthed. "Talk to you later."

I didn't catch up with her until lunchtime. We're in different sets for English and maths, so I had to wait all morning to find out what the note said and why she'd come in looking so het up. I grabbed a sandwich and went over to where the others were sitting.

"I know why Crystal's not getting married!" Ellie blurted out before I'd even sat down. "Look!" She took a newspaper out of her bag and pointed to a tiny article at the bottom of the entertainment pages. The headline said:

GARLIC PICKERS TO PLAY ON MALONE'S
SPECIAL DAY

"No way," I breathed, scanning the article. Suddenly it all made sense. Sophia Malone had asked The Garlic Pickers to play a special set at her wedding. That must've been what the meeting was about that day I was in the park with Crystal. And that was obviously why they'd postponed their own wedding. There's no way Crystal would let Tyler miss an opportunity like that.

"What are you actually talking about?" said Phoebe. "We haven't got a clue, have we, Polly?" Polly shook her head.

I filled them in on the whole story. From when Crystal's invitation arrived until the other day when Mum found it under my pillow. I explained about Crystal and Tyler's wedding *and* Sophia Malone's wedding and how they were both on the same day. "Crystal bought me a dress and everything," I said. "This awful pink tutu thing that itches like crazy."

"Never mind about your itchy dress!"

shrieked Polly. "Are you telling me that your sister is going out with someone from The Garlic Pickers and you never told us?"

I shook my head, shrugging. "He was just Crystal's boyfriend and they hadn't even been together for that long when she moved out."

"But you know what this means, don't you?" said Ellie. We all looked at her. "Your mum and Tyler will both be at the wedding and if you're there as well you could do something to get them talking. Get your Mum to realize that Crystal and Tyler are serious."

"Yeah, and maybe you could get me an autograph at the same time," said Polly. "The drummer in The Garlic Pickers is really hot."

"Ellie, you're a genius!" I said, ignoring Polly. "That's exactly what I've got to do. Crystal might be there as well and if she is it'll be the perfect place to get Mum to see that's she's been wrong about them all along."

"Why don't we *all* come and help your mum with the flowers?" said Polly. "We wouldn't even care if we got paid, would we, Phoebs?"

"Not if we got to meet The Garlic Pickers!" said Phoebe. "We'd actually pay *her*!"

"You guys – this is serious!" I said, but I couldn't help grinning.

"I think it's really romantic anyway," said Ellie. "Crystal and Tyler getting married and him being in a band – it's like out of the movies or something."

I glanced at Ellie. "Talking of romantic, we haven't told them about Arthur and Mrs. Beagle."

Phoebe and Polly practically wet themselves as I described Arthur practising his proposal. "Honestly, it's the funniest thing I've ever heard," Polly spluttered. "Especially as Mandy is convinced Arthur is in love with *her*."

It was so brilliant to be laughing and mucking about all together after the last few weeks. I was never going to fall out with Ellie again, no matter what.

"Listen, Sam, I am so sorry about the detention," she said as we made our way back to class. "I always read the entertainment pages while I'm eating breakfast and I saw that article and I thought I was going to burst if I didn't tell you."

"It's okay, Ellie. In fact it couldn't be better. Well, as long as my mum doesn't find out!"

17
The Worst News Ever!

But of course Mum *did* find out. I don't know how I ever thought I was going to hide it from her. Madame Blanc always calls the parents to let them know she's keeping their child late at school so Mum knew all about the detention before I even got home that day. It's not like I could talk my way out of it either because I wasn't about to tell her about Ellie and the newspaper article and how The Garlic Pickers had been asked to play at Sophia Malone's wedding.

She called me into the kitchen the second I walked through the door. She was sitting at the table with her head in her hands, as if she'd just heard someone had died or something.

"A detention, Sam! I'm so disappointed. Honestly, what were you doing?"

"I didn't do anything. Madame Blanc caught Ellie passing me a note, but it was nothing to do with me. I didn't even see what the note said." I dropped my bag on the floor and sank down into a chair.

"*Passing notes!* For goodness' sake – how old are you? And you've always been so good at languages. Don't you like French any more?"

"I do, Mum. I love French, but Madame Blanc is so strict you only have to breathe and she's on your case."

Mum rolled her eyes. "But you promised me you were taking your work seriously this year..."

"I am, Mum. I'm trying *so* hard..."

She waved her arm at me as if she didn't want to hear any more. "Well, anyway, I've made an appointment with your form teacher."

"What do you mean?" I could feel the colour drain out of my face.

"It's nothing to get worked up about. I just want to find out what's really going on."

"What are you talking about? There's nothing *going on*. I'm working so hard and I'm actually in the top set for all my core subjects." I glared at her across the table. "When is the meeting anyway?"

"It's next Friday morning, but I don't want you fretting about it all week. If you're doing as well as you say you are then you've got nothing to be worried about, have you?"

But I *was* worried. Mum was on the warpath. She was desperate to find a reason to stop me going to drama and getting this detention could easily be it. Ellie was gutted when I told her the next morning. "It's all my fault," she wailed. "Why don't I ever think before I do things?"

"Don't be stupid. If you hadn't seen the article I wouldn't even know The Garlic Pickers were going to be at the wedding."

"What do you think Mr. Bayliss will say anyway? It's not like you've been in loads of trouble or anything."

"I know, but remember I told you my mum's been dying to get me this tutor who only has a Saturday slot? Well, I swear this is going to be all the excuse she needs."

I couldn't stop thinking about it the next day at drama. I knew my lines inside out, but I was so worried about the meeting I kept losing track of where we were. Mandy was standing in front of the stage encouraging us to speak out and stay in character, and all I could think about was how this could be my last show ever at Star Makers. There just didn't seem to be much point if Mum was going to stop me coming anyway.

"What's going on, Sam?" said Mandy. "You've been so good with your lines up until now."

"It's not the lines," I muttered. "It's just other stuff."

"I bet *I* know what it is," said Sara.

I gave her a look. "No, you don't."

Suddenly Monty B leaped onto the stage, landing right in front of me. "Detective Biscuit's on the case, he'll soon sort out your gloomy face."

"It wouldn't *be* gloomy if you'd just get *out* of my face."

"Don't start arguing again, *please*," said Mandy. "Remember how we're all supposed to be pulling together as a team."

"Oh, I know, let's do some more of those trust games," Sara piped up.

"Er...let's not," I said. "Anyway I'm fine now."

We started the scene again and somehow I managed to keep up with where we were. I loved being Laura. In fact, I loved everything about the show. Mum might think acting was just a hobby, but it meant the world to me. The only downer was that I had to do most of my scenes with Adam – but it's not like we had to kiss onstage or anything embarrassing like that. And anyway, my latest strategy of Ignoring Him Completely seemed to be working quite well.

The scene we were practising was my favourite in the whole show. It's when Laura finally solves the mystery of the phantom face. Detective Biscuit keeps saying that April *must* have come to a sorry end and the butler *must* be guilty, even though he swears blind he wasn't there the day she went missing. But Laura works out that the butler has an identical twin brother who April was madly in love with and that they'd run off together. That's why it seemed as if the butler was in two places at the same time.

"Hang on," said Monty B as the scene finished. "I was just about to work that out myself, wasn't I, Phoebs?"

"What are you talking about?" said Phoebe.

Monty B waved his notebook at her. "You know, all the clues we collected and—"

"Oh my God, yeah," said Neesha, "you do realize this isn't real? That you're not *really* collecting clues."

"I might be," said Monty B. "I *am* a detective, you know."

Neesha rolled her eyes. "Can someone please tell him it's only a play."

"But break it to him gently," said Adam. "You don't want to shatter all his illusions. It's like telling someone that there's no such thing as fairies!"

"What do you mean?" cried Sara, turning pink.

"She still believes in fairies, I'm afraid," said Phoebe. "And the man in the moon!"

Sara opened her mouth to say something but Mandy held up her hand. "Enough!" she said. "I want you to all start taking this seriously. The dress rehearsal is in two weeks' time and there's still so much to do."

Two weeks? My brain went into overdrive. The wedding was in two weeks. How could the wedding *and* the dress rehearsal both be on the same day? It was crazy. I'd known the dress rehearsal was coming up, obviously, but I must've blocked the exact date out of my mind!

Mandy took a deep breath. "Look, let's have a quick break and then I want you all back onstage – and I want you focused!"

I went to grab my stuff from the front of the stage, but Mandy called me over to the piano.

"Do you want to talk about what's worrying you, Sam? It would be such a shame if something outside drama affected your performance – especially since you've got such a big part."

I shook my head. "It's okay. I know all my lines. I won't let you down."

"I know you won't, sweetheart. That's not what I meant. It's just that you seem to have lost some of your confidence lately, that's all."

I thought about the wedding and Crystal, and the detention and the tutor. I could've told Mandy, I suppose, and got her to talk to Mum, but I knew it wouldn't make the slightest difference. Mum just didn't get how important acting was to me and she never would.

I started to make up some rubbish about having too much homework, but then Arthur burst in, looking very flustered.

"Oh hello, Mandy my dear, you haven't seen June this morning, have you?"

Mandy shook her head. "Sorry, Arthur, you've lost me."

"June Beagle? Mrs. Beagle? You remember."

Mandy sighed. "Oh yes, Mrs. Beagle. I didn't realize her first name was June."

"Oh yes...June by name, June by nature," said Arthur.

"Are you okay, Arthur?" said Mandy, looking at him strangely.

"Top of the world, Mandy. But if you do happen to see her at any point, please could you mention that I was looking for her? Church business," he added, tapping his nose.

Mandy nodded and turned back to me, trying to keep a straight face.

"Now where were we, Sam?"

"Don't worry, Mandy. I'll just go off and practise the next scene so I don't mess up again later."

I scooted back over to the others before she could say anything. If Mum decided to stop me coming to Star Makers, there was nothing Mandy could do about it.

"What did Arthur want?" said Ellie.

"He was looking for June. That's Mrs. Beagle's first name apparently."

"Hey, I bet when we come back next term they'll be engaged or married or something,"

said Phoebe. They all burst out laughing but I suddenly felt sick to my stomach. If Mum decided I needed The Great Mrs. Raja on Saturday mornings I wouldn't even *be* here next term.

I tried much harder for the rest of the session. I wanted to show Mandy how well I could do, even if it did end up being my last show. We just about managed to get to the end of Act Two and she was thrilled. "It still needs some work but it was *so* much better. I don't know what you ate at break, Sam, but it certainly gave you the boost you needed."

"It's got nothing to do with what she ate, it's being onstage with *me* that does it," joked Adam. He went to throw his arm round my shoulder but I ducked out of the way, blushing. It was very difficult to Ignore Him Completely when he was that close. In fact, it was pretty much impossible.

"Come on, Sam," said Ellie, linking arms as

we left the hall. "You were amazing and it's got nothing to do with what you ate – *or* being onstage with Adam Dale. He's just a lemon – remember?"

Crystal finally called me on Wednesday, ten whole days after Dad had gone round there. She didn't mention the wedding, or Mum and Dad, or the fact that I'd left about twenty million messages on her phone.

"I really want to show you something," she trilled. "Will you meet me down by the swings after school?"

I was supposed to be going straight home to do my homework – Mum's orders! But Crystal sounded so excited and I was so desperate to see her, it was difficult to say no. I had to make sure she wasn't angry about Mum finding the wedding invitation – that she didn't blame me in some way. She was already there when I arrived, pacing around the playground like a caged lion. "Hey, Sam." She gave me a quick hug. "Come and take a look at this." She pulled me over to a bench. "Remember I told you about that meeting Tyler had with his agent – well, he's only going to be playing a set at Sophia Malone's wedding next Saturday!"

"No way! That's amazing," I said, pretending to be really surprised.

"So anyway," she went on, "I decided to make a silver candle holder with crystals studded all the way round the edge, to, you know, go on the tables at the wedding. I just thought it was the sort of thing Sophia Malone would like. I never thought for a second that anything would come of it, but I sent it off to her agent and Tyler put in a good word for me and basically she thought it was fantastic. She's asked me to make twenty – one for each table. Can you believe it?"

She pulled out one of the candleholders

from her bag and held it out to show me. It was easily the most beautiful thing I'd ever seen.

"Crystal this is incredible." I couldn't get over it. "You mean these are actually going to be on the tables at Sophia Malone's wedding?"

"Yes, I know, it's crazy!" she laughed. "*Crystal's Crystals* at Sophia Malone's wedding!"

"So will you actually be there on the day?"

She nodded, her eyes shining. "Not because of the candleholders or anything, I'm just going along with the band."

My heart started to race. "So you'll definitely be there, at the wedding, with Tyler?"

"I know, it's wicked, isn't it? Me at Sophia Malone's wedding!"

It was more than wicked. It was literally the answer to my prayers. Finally I had a way to get Mum and Crystal in the same room together. And if they were at a wedding, especially such an *important* wedding, and they came face-to-face, it's not like they'd be able to get into a big fight or start screaming at each other or anything stupid like that. Not when Mum was trying to impress with her flowers and Crystal with her candleholders. It was the perfect place for them to make up.

"This one's extra by the way," said Crystal, pressing the candle holder into my hand. "I made it for you."

I felt tears spring to my eyes.

"It's okay," she said, giving me a hug. "I know it wasn't your fault about the invitation. And it's not your fault that Mum's the way she is."

I ran my hands around the candle holder. It was so sparkly and precious. Exactly like Crystal. "You will make up with Mum, you know," I said. "You can't stay angry with each other for ever."

She shrugged and looked away, but not before I saw the hurt in her eyes.

A History Lesson!

I felt so much better after seeing Crystal, but I was still dreading Friday and Mum's meeting with Mr. Bayliss. I worked extra-hard all week but I knew it wouldn't make the slightest difference. I quite like Mr. Bayliss, but he's mega-strict. He's always harping on about how we need to **Make The Most Of The Opportunities Presented To Us** – just like Mum really. What *was* it about grown-ups and the word "opportunities"? If I had my way, I'd ban it!

I dawdled home as slowly as I possibly could on Friday afternoon. I made up this stupid game where I was only allowed to take another step forward every time three cars drove past. I was desperately hoping that Mum might have gone straight back to the shop after the meeting, but when I eventually made it home she was already there waiting for me. I stood for a second in the hall, bracing myself.

"Sam Lester!" she called out from the kitchen. "I am *so* proud of you I could burst!"

"*What*?" I dropped my bag by the door and ran in to find her.

"I've had the most brilliant meeting with Mr. Bayliss," she gushed, pouring me a cup of tea and cutting a huge slice of lemon cake. She was so excited her hands were trembling. "He's really impressed with you, Sam. He thinks you've got great potential. He *thinks* that if you set your mind to it you could go to one of the top universities – Oxford or Cambridge even!"

Mum's eyes were shining. It was like Crystal all over again. Except I wasn't even thirteen yet and it was years until I had to worry about which university I should go to. I actually had my heart set on going to drama school; one of the really good ones in London. But I could just imagine how that would go down.

"So anyway," Mum was saying, "I'm not going to stop you going to Star Makers this term, obviously, but I've called Mrs. Raja and she's perfectly happy for you to start straight after Christmas. Two hours of tutoring every Saturday from ten till twelve. This is such a fantastic opportunity for you, Sam. You're doing so well and I just want to make sure you keep up your grades." Mum plonked another slice of cake on my plate, as if stuffing me full of treats would make up for what she was saying.

"I can't go to a tutor on Saturday mornings," I said, pushing my plate away. "You know I can't."

"Look, I'm not going to stop you acting, Sam. I know how much it means to you and everyone needs their hobbies. But you'll just have to find a drama club that runs on a different day – that's not so unreasonable, is it?"

It was like my worst nightmare. I was actually being punished for doing well at school.

"I'm not giving up Star Makers!" I yelled, squaring up to Mum. "And stop calling it a hobby! It is NOT a hobby. I don't care how brilliant Mrs. Raja is – you'll have to find a different tutor if you're so set on me having one. Not that you ever seemed that bothered about it when Crystal was here!"

Mum got that look on her face. **THE CRYSTAL LOOK**. "This has got nothing to do with her," she snapped. She grabbed a cloth and started to clear away the cake.

"Yes it has! It's got *everything* to do with her." I was spitting mad now. "Before Crystal left you were busy controlling *her* life and now she's gone you're trying to control *mine*!"

Mum whipped round. "It's not like that!" she

said. "I don't want to control your life, I just want you to do the best you can."

"But Mum, I don't need a tutor. You heard what Mr. Bayliss said – I'm doing really well already. And I'll work even harder, I swear."

Mum took a deep breath, closing her eyes. "Just listen to me a minute, Sam, will you? You've no idea what it was like when Crystal was a baby." She stopped for a second, letting her breath out slowly. I was about to ask what Crystal being a baby had to do with me and Mrs. Raja, but she carried on before I could say anything. "*Everyone* thought I'd be a terrible mum; that I was far too young and immature. People used to look down their noses at me. They all said I was selfish and irresponsible, including my own family. They said I wasn't fit to be a mother, but I proved them wrong, every single one of them." She twisted the dishcloth round and round her hand, staring off into the distance.

"Crystal was always streets ahead of the other children. She was the first in her class to read and she always came top in everything. I used to take her to the library and to all the museums and art galleries. I wanted to give her every chance to succeed and I'm going to do the same for you. *No one's* going to say I didn't do the best for my girls."

"But that was ages ago, Mum. You don't have to prove anything to anyone now." But even as I said the words I knew in Mum's mind she did. In Mum's mind all those people who thought she'd be rubbish were still there, waiting for her to mess up.

She finished clearing up and pulled on her coat. "Look, I'm going back to the shop. I've still got deliveries to get ready for tomorrow and I've got a big meeting on Monday with Lavender. It's just over a week until the wedding and Sophia still keeps changing her mind."

I sat in the kitchen for ages thinking about

what Mum had said. I could see how difficult it must've been for her back then, but however bad it was, it didn't give her the right to ruin *my* life now. Somehow I had to make her see that being serious about acting was just as important as being serious about English or maths or any of the other subjects we do at school. I had to prove myself to *her*, just like she felt she had to prove herself to all those stupid people who treated her so badly when Crystal was a baby.

"I hear we've got a genius in the family!" Dad shouted up when he got in from work. I was in my room sulking and the last thing I wanted to talk about was Mum's meeting with Mr. Bayliss and how clever I was supposed to be. A few seconds later he came bursting into my room, grinning like an idiot.

"I Am Not A Genius, Dad! I've only been working hard to get Mum off my case, but it's totally backfired."

He came over and sat on my bed. "She's just proud of you, sweetheart. You know what she's like."

"Yes, but what about what *I'm* like?" I muttered. "She thinks I'm going to be the next prime minister or something, but she never actually listens to what *I* want to do with my life. And how about you? I bet you never really wanted to work in a bank."

"What do you mean?" said Dad, surprised. "I really enjoy my job, you know."

"Yes, but I bet you didn't want to work in a bank when you were at school and you had dreams." I took a deep breath. "I know about the band, Dad. Aunty Mags told me. I've seen all the old newspaper cuttings. You could've been *really* big!"

Dad laughed and pulled me into his arms for a hug. "Yes, we could've been big – we had some good reviews – but there are no guarantees in the music business. And anyway, you can't go touring round in a band when you've got a young family to look after."

"But, Dad, you *must* regret leaving. I mean if you don't regret it, why didn't you ever tell us? Why have you kept Stevie and the Stingrays a secret for all these years?" I pulled away from him so I could look into his eyes and see if he was being honest.

"I do miss it sometimes," he said. "We had such a laugh together. But I don't *regret* it – not when I look at you and Crystal. If I'd stayed on with the band I would've been one of those dads who's never around for his kids. I would've missed your birthdays and Christmas and half your school plays. That wasn't the life for me. Perhaps I just didn't want it enough."

"So why didn't you tell us then?" I said, determined to find out the truth. "If you don't regret leaving, why have you kept it secret? You never play the guitar any more – I don't even know if you've got one."

Dad stood up to go downstairs. "I have got a guitar," he said at the door. He stopped for a second with his head tipped to one side, thinking. "I only stopped playing it because it upset your mum so much."

"What do you mean?"

Dad shrugged. "She feels guilty," he said. "She still feels guilty about me leaving the band, even though I've told her a million times over that if I had to do it all again I'd make the same decision today that I made twenty years ago."

"But, Dad, have you actually asked Mum if she still feels like that now? Because honestly, I can't bear the thought of your guitar stuffed in a cupboard somewhere. It just doesn't seem right."

"We don't really talk about it any more, Sam. It's ancient history. You know, it's almost as if the band and everything happened to someone else."

"But it's not too late is it?" I went over to

him and wrapped my arms round his middle. "You could still play now, couldn't you?"

Dad smiled. "What, at my age?"

"I don't mean in a band or anything, but you could still play. You *should* play, whatever Mum thinks."

Dad gave me the tightest hug. "You hang on to your dreams, Sam," he said. "Hang on to your dreams, no matter what."

"I'm trying," I said, hugging him back. "But will you please talk to Mum about Mrs. Raja? Just explain to her that I have to stay at Star Makers. There must be other tutors I could go to, after school or on Sundays."

Dad unwrapped my arms and backed out of the door. "I'll do my best, sweetheart," he said. "Promise."

I stayed in my room for the rest of the evening, trying to work out what I was going to do. It felt like there was so much stuff going on in the family – stuff that had started before

Crystal was even born. Dad feeling bad because Mum had given up her place at university and Mum feeling guilty because Dad had left the band. Our history teacher at school is always saying *You can't go back and change the past, you can only learn lessons from it* – if only I could get Mum and Dad to realize that before Mum came face-to-face with Crystal at Sophia Malone's wedding.

I was still lying there, stewing over the whole sorry mess, when Ellie called.

"You'll never guess what," she said. "I've just found Eddie's sweatshirt. It was only *in the freezer!*"

I shook my head, smiling. "Ellie, I'm not even going to ask you why..."

"No, seriously, I know it sounds completely mad but it was weeks and weeks ago and I was practising one of the dances from the show and I remember I was so hot I thought I was going to die and—"

"Don't tell me...you froze Eddie's sweatshirt to help you cool down."

"Well, I was only going to pop it in there for five minutes but I must've forgotten and then Mum found it today when she took out some pork chops for supper."

"At least you didn't put it in the oven," I said, giggling. "Is it ruined?"

"No it's fine, actually. I've defrosted it and it's just a bit damp and smelly. Anyway, how did your mum's meeting with Mr. Bayliss go?"

"Erm...he thinks I'm a genius so Mum says I've got to have this tutor so I can go to some posh university and the only time the tutor can see me is on Saturday mornings."

"But that's just crazy!" Ellie wailed down the phone. "What are you going to do?"

"I don't know. All I keep thinking is that everything would be okay if I could just get my mum and Crystal to sort things out at the wedding."

"Yes, but *how* exactly?"

"I don't know that either," I admitted, "but I've basically got a week to come up with a totally foolproof plan."

"I'll think as well," said Ellie, "and we'll talk tomorrow."

We didn't get much chance to talk the next day. It was the last rehearsal before the dress rehearsal and Mandy was in Serious Mode. We sang through all the songs and then spent ages working out the finale and bows. I had to run on right at the end and take my bow with Adam, but it wasn't as bad as I thought it was going to be. That's one of the things I love most about acting – the second I get onstage I kind of forget about everything else, including the fact that I'm standing there holding hands with Adam Dale!

The next week crawled by. I didn't speak to Crystal – and Mum was at work 24/7, sorting out the flowers for Saturday. Sophia Malone had finally decided on a "theme" and Mum had been working flat out to get everything ready in time. I spent loads of time with Dad, but he didn't mention his guitar or the band and I didn't really feel like bringing it up again.

I practised my lines for the show every day after school and lay in bed every night working on my plan for the wedding. I desperately needed Mum and Crystal to make up and not just so I could stay at Star Makers. What I wanted most of all was for Crystal to come home. But what if she refused to talk to Mum at the wedding? What if she told Mum to get lost and walked out all over again?

19
The Wedding

I woke up on Saturday the 28th of November with about a million butterflies flapping about inside my stomach. It was the dress rehearsal *and* the wedding and it felt as if my whole future was at stake. I'd told Mum there was no way I could miss drama on such an important day, so she'd arranged for Aunty Mags to pick me up at one o'clock and drive me straight over to the reception hall.

Ellie came over after breakfast and we got the bus up to drama. I felt a bit sick about the dress rehearsal. It's usually so exciting to see our costumes for the first time and do a proper run-through without stopping – but I was just so worried about everything else that was going on. I'd tried talking to Mum about how much I wanted to stay at Star Makers, but she just said, "I should've realized all along that Crystal was the creative one and you were the one with all the brains!"

I could've pointed out that Crystal had to be pretty clever to be running her own business at eighteen years old – and that acting was just as creative as making jewellery – but somewhere along the line she had decided that The Great Mrs. Raja was the answer to all her problems and nothing I said was going to make the slightest difference.

"Has your mum mentioned that tutor again?" said Ellie. I was testing her on her lines while we waited for the bus.

I shook my head. "She hasn't exactly mentioned her – but then we're not really talking."

"But how are you going to help her at the wedding if you're ignoring each other?"

"We *are* talking when we need to, but things are pretty frosty between us."

"Like Eddie's sweatshirt, you mean?" said Ellie.

I smiled. "Erm…kind of. Anyway I've been working on this plan all week, you know, for getting Mum and Crystal together at the wedding. I'm pretty certain that if they make up, Mum won't be so bothered about getting me a tutor. She's only got herself in a state about my education because Crystal turned down her place at uni."

Ellie leaned towards me. "So what are you going to do then? Lock them in a room together?"

I stared at her.

Ellie's mouth dropped open. "You're not serious."

"I am. Deadly."

"But *Sam*! What if it doesn't work? What if there are no locks on the doors or they're never in the same room at the same time? Or Crystal storms out? Or—"

"Okay, I get the picture! Look, I don't know what I'll do if it doesn't work. It's *got* to work because if it doesn't my mum will force me to leave Star Makers and I'll never, ever forgive her."

"Neither will I," said Ellie.

The bus took ages and by the time we arrived everyone was already there, crowded around Sandeep.

"Look, you two!" he shouted, holding up his leg. "No cast!"

"That's brilliant!" cried Ellie. "And your leg looks exactly the same as it did before!"

"What do you mean? What did you think it was going to look like?"

"Oh, it's just that I had this dream the other night that when you had your cast taken off your leg had mutated into two legs, so altogether you had three."

"Is she okay?" said Sandeep to me, but just

then Julian called him over to sort out the sound. Julian couldn't come to the actual show because he was working somewhere else that night, so this was his last chance to make sure Sandeep knew what he was doing.

"Come on, girls," said Mandy, handing us a pile of clothes. "Costumes on."

My costume was pretty ordinary – just a plain skirt and shirt – but some of the others were amazing. Monty B was wearing this old-fashioned detective's outfit – sort of like Sherlock Holmes. He came rushing back from the toilets and then stood in the middle of the hall for ages, trying to look at himself in his huge magnifying glass.

"For goodness sake, Digestive Biscuit! Stop admiring yourself," said Phoebe.

"I can't help it," said Monty B. "I just look so...so...I can't think of the word..."

"Neither can I," said Adam. "Oh yes I can – it's 'stupid'."

Everyone burst out laughing, but I didn't really feel like joining in. I was too worried about the wedding and my plan and how *The Phantom Face* might be my last ever show at Star Makers. It was the same when we started the rehearsal. Mandy kept asking me to put more effort into my performance and even Sara started moaning about it – as if she was the assistant director or something.

"It's not because you've got a crush on someone, is it?" she said, staring right at Adam in the most obvious way imaginable.

"I'm afraid it is," said Monty B before I could say anything or push her off the stage. "She can't help it, Sara. It's just the effect I have on women."

"In your dreams," said Adam.

"I actually had this dream," said Ellie, "and—"

"Not now!" cried Mandy. "It's the dress rehearsal. Come on, Sam. I can see you know

 269

all your lines and all your cues, but could you please just put a bit more spark into it?"

It was so frustrating, because I desperately wanted to show Mandy how good I was, but I seemed to be getting worse by the minute. How was I supposed to prove to Mum how serious I was about acting if she came to see me in the show and I was rubbish? And if she hadn't made up with Crystal by then, would it make any difference anyway?

We started again from the beginning but we didn't get very far because the eerie music kept playing out at the wrong time. "Don't worry, Mandy," said Sandeep. "I'm just getting used to the equipment. It'll be fine by next week."

Mandy sighed. "I really hope you're right, because I'm beginning to get that feeling of doom I always get just before a show. You know, that everything's going to go wrong."

Right that second, as if on cue, Arthur came in.

"Oh hello, Mandy. I can see you're busy, my dear, but we never did have that little chat in the end, did we?"

"No, we didn't," said Mandy, firmly. "But I'm sure there'll be plenty of time *after* the show."

"It honestly won't take a moment," said Arthur. "It's just about your...ahem...lovely long hair..." He paused for a minute and Mandy jumped up.

"I'm sorry, Arthur, but this really isn't the time or the place," she said, and she ushered him out of the hall as quickly as she could, shutting the door firmly behind him.

"What's he going on about her hair for?" I said to Ellie.

She shrugged, giggling. "Beats me. Maybe he wants Mrs. Beagle to get hair extensions or something?"

After a lot of stopping and starting we finally managed to run right through the show – *with*

the sound effects and projected images – and it actually went pretty well.

"That was great!" cried Mandy as we finished the finale. "I take it all back, guys. This is easily going to be the best show ever!"

"You always say that," said Monty B. "But they can't *all* be the best, can they? You know, technically speaking…"

"Haven't you got a crime to solve or something?" said Neesha. "You know, *technically speaking.*"

We all spilled out of the hall, laughing. Aunty Mags was waiting for me downstairs with Riley. He bounded straight over to Adam as if he actually remembered him, and Adam seemed just as happy to see Riley.

"How's he getting on?" he said, heaving Riley up into his arms.

Aunty Mags rolled her eyes. "Well, if I said he's the naughtiest dog I've ever had in my life I wouldn't be exaggerating!" she laughed. "He's starting his obedience lessons on Monday and he's going to be in for a big shock."

I went over to say bye to the others while Adam and Aunty Mags were chatting.

"Don't forget to text us," said Ellie, giving me a hug. "We're all going back to mine and we'll be desperate for news."

I've been to a few weddings before but I've never been to *anything* like Sophia Malone's wedding. When we arrived at the hall – which was actually one of those very posh houses that you could easily spend the whole day looking round – the grounds were filled with sleek, black limousines and about a hundred guys with cameras. The second we stopped the car they began to shout out to us, as if *we* were the celebrities and they wanted to snap *our* picture.

"Wow! Hasn't your mum done well for

herself, landing a job like this?" said Aunty Mags. *And Crystal*, I thought, but I didn't say anything.

An important-looking man with a clipboard came bustling over to the car and when we showed him our passes and said we were there to do the flowers he rushed us through a side entrance, quite a way from where the other guests were going in. I said goodbye to Aunty Mags and the man led me down a grand corridor with shiny floors and old-fashioned portraits, all the way along to where Mum was waiting for me in the main dining room.

I stood in the doorway with my mouth hanging open. It was the most romantic room I'd ever seen in my life. There was a huge chandelier in the middle of the ceiling, dripping with thousands of tiny crystals. The light shimmering through the glass made a pattern of sparkly dots on every wall – kind of like a giant disco ball. I was dying to take a picture and send it to Ellie and the others – they wouldn't believe it.

Mum was busy sorting out the table arrangements. She'd used bendy wire and delicate red flowers to create the shape of two entwined hearts. There was also a flickering red candle sitting in one of Crystal's candleholders on each of the tables. Of course Mum didn't have the slightest clue that Crystal had made the candleholders, but the overall effect was stunning.

"The tables look amazing, Mum," I said. "How did you ever get the idea?"

Mum smiled. She was probably relieved I wasn't giving her the frosty treatment. "Well, Sophia finally decided that she wanted the theme to be love hearts and I thought two hearts would look much prettier than one. Lavender told me there were going to be candles, so I tried out all different ways of arranging the hearts around the candle and I thought this way would be best."

"Have you seen Lavender yet?" I asked as casually as I could. "Or anyone else?"

Mum shook her head. "They've pretty much left me to it. The band have been in and out, setting up, but I haven't seen Lavender."

It was crazy. Tyler had probably walked straight past Mum – maybe they'd even said hi – but because she'd always been so set against meeting him properly, neither of them would have had a clue.

"Are you going to give me a hand then, Sam? Myra and Keeley were fantastic this morning but they had to get back to the shop to do the normal Saturday orders."

"What was it like at the church?"

"I didn't see the service or anything. We'd finished before Sophia or any of the guests arrived and then I came straight here to start the tables. Listen, why don't you pass me the wire and cutters as we go around? I'm so nervous it's taking me twice as long as I thought it would."

I was nervous too. Very. My hands were slippy on the cutters and the butterflies were back in my stomach but a hundred times worse than this morning. What if Crystal didn't show up *before* the wedding? What if they never actually came face-to-face at all? I didn't know whether to tell Mum about the candleholders or just wait and see what happened. My whole plan to get them together suddenly seemed rubbish. It wasn't a proper plan at all. A door banged down the corridor, and then another. My stomach lurched, but no one came into the hall.

We worked on for a bit and then Mum stood back to check the table we'd just finished. "Do you think the hearts look obvious enough?" she said. "I didn't want to go too over the top, so I've tried to make them as dainty as possible but…"

"The hearts look brilliant," I gushed, "*and*

the candleholders." I *had* to say something. I had no idea where Crystal was and time was ticking by. "They're beautiful as well, aren't they?" I held my breath, waiting to see what she would say.

"Yes, they're lovely," she agreed. "I might actually ask Lavender who made them – it would be great to get some to sell in *Everything's Rosy*. They'd look a treat dotted around the shop."

This was my chance. "Well, you'll never believe it, Mum," I started, forcing the words out before I lost my nerve, "but I actually know who..." There was a sudden noise by the door and we both swung round. It was Crystal. She was standing there with her hands on her hips and her chin jutting out.

"I made them," she said. "The candleholders are mine. *I* made them."

Mum dropped the flower she was holding and literally stepped back in shock. She looked from me to Crystal and back to me again. I could just imagine what she was thinking.

"What's going on?" she said in the end. "Did you know about this, Sam?"

I suddenly realized I was still holding my breath. I couldn't believe I actually thought this was going to be a good idea. I must've been mad.

"It's got nothing to do with Sam," said Crystal, jutting her chin out even further. "Sophia Malone asked me to make the candleholders for the tables, but I didn't know *you* were doing the flowers."

She spun round and started to walk out of the room.

"Wait!" said Mum. "Let's talk...can't we just talk, Crystal, *please*?"

"What's left to say?" said Crystal. She turned back, her eyes glittering. "I'm pretty sure you said everything you wanted to say to me on the night of my birthday."

Mum took a step towards her. "Look, I know you're upset, Crystal, but I didn't mean to hurt you. It's just that I had all these dreams for you..."

Crystal shook her head. "But it wasn't about *my* dreams, was it, Mum? It was about yours. It was about me coming along eighteen years ago and ruining all *your* dreams. I was just One Big Mistake, wasn't I? Isn't that what you said? That you didn't want me to make the same mistake you made."

"But I didn't mean *you!*" cried Mum. "You and Sam – you're my special girls..."

"*Special,*" spat Crystal. "You didn't make me feel very special that night, did you? What do you think it feels like when your own mother says she wishes you'd never been born?"

Mum lurched towards Crystal. "*I didn't...*" she gasped. "*I...*" Her voice broke and she started to cry.

"Look, this is stupid," said Crystal, but her

eyes were bright too. "They're going to be bringing the guests in soon and you haven't even finished the flowers, and anyway I've got to get back to Tyler and the guys. If you've got something to say to me, it'll have to wait."

"What do you mean, Tyler and the guys?" croaked Mum.

"Oh sorry, I forgot to mention," said Crystal. "My *loser* boyfriend is playing a gig at the celebrity wedding of the year...guess he's not such a loser *after all*!"

"But she doesn't think he's a loser!" I cried out in desperation. I couldn't keep quiet a second longer. "She fell in love with a musician herself. Didn't you, Mum?"

20
The Biggest Challenge Yet...

Mum froze.

"What the hell are you talking about?" said Crystal.

"It's true," I said, the words tumbling out. "Dad used to play in a band and Mum came to see him in a gig and they fell in love and that was way before he got a job in a bank. Tell her, Mum. Tell her it's true."

"What a load of rubbish!" snapped Crystal.

"Come on, Mum. Tell her about Stevie and the Stingrays. Dad was in a band, just like Tyler, and it didn't stop you falling for him."

But Mum just stood there, speechless.

"I don't know what you're on about, Sam,"

said Crystal, "but whatever it is, I really couldn't care less. I know you're just trying to help, but it's too late!" And she flounced out of the room, just like she always does when she wants to get the last word.

"She's right," sobbed Mum. "It's too late." She sank down onto a chair and put her head in her hands.

"Come on," I said, before she lost it altogether. "Crystal's right, let's get the flowers sorted, at least."

I managed to get her up and we worked really hard together until the tables were finished. I could see her hands shaking like mad as she clipped and shaped the flowers, and every few minutes a huge tear ran down her face, but she didn't say a word. We were just packing up when Lavender came in.

"Oh darlings, it's absolutely stunning," she cried. "And who would've thought the little candleholders and the flowers shaped like hearts would come together so perfectly. They're quite simply a match made in heaven."

In hell, more like, I thought, as I texted Ellie and the others that everything had gone completely wrong.

Lavender ushered us into a sort of small waiting room near the hall. She said she needed to bring some forms for Mum to sign and she hurried off down the corridor.

We'd been sitting there for about fifteen minutes when the music started. I went to stand by the open door and peered round so I could just about see into the hall. All the guests had arrived. The room was packed full of beautiful women, and men in their smartest suits, all sipping champagne and looking outrageously glamorous. The Garlic Pickers were standing on the stage at the far end. Tyler was right in the middle and he was singing directly to Sophia Malone. The lyrics were quite simple, but it was such a romantic song.

"He wrote it for me," said Crystal, coming up alongside me. "It's called 'Precious Girl' and he wrote it for me when I moved in with him. *He* thinks I'm special even if my own mother doesn't."

"You are special," said Mum quietly, coming out of the room. She held her hands out to Crystal, pleading. "You're *my* precious girl and if I *ever* made you feel that you weren't wanted then I am so, so sorry. I'd do anything to take back what I said that night, Crystal. You've got to believe me. *Anything.*"

Tears started to run down Crystal's face. "But you *said* you didn't want me," she sobbed, crumbling suddenly. "You said giving up your place at university was the biggest mistake of your life – and we all know why you had to give it up…"

"But I didn't mean—"

"You did!" cried Crystal. "You gave up everything for me. I ruined your life. That's

what you meant when you said—"

"No," said Mum firmly, pulling Crystal into her arms. "That's *not* what I meant. Having you was the best decision I've *ever* made in my life and I couldn't love you more or be prouder of you. I think you're incredible."

I started crying as well then, it was just too much.

And then Lavender arrived with the forms. "Oh darlings," she gasped, looking a bit flustered. "Does anyone need a tissue?"

Mum was very quiet on the way home. I kind of thought she'd be over the moon, but I guess six months of upset and rows don't just evaporate into thin air.

"I'm so tired," she said as we drew up outside the house. "I don't think I've ever been this tired in my life."

"Well, Mum, you have just done the flowers

for Sophia Malone's wedding *and* made up with Crystal."

I was so fed up with hiding things – I wasn't about to pretend the big teary scene had never happened.

"Yes, *and* made up with Crystal," said Mum, and she didn't even seem cross that I'd brought it up. "I'm grateful, Sam; so grateful that I got the chance to say sorry. I should've listened to Crystal *and* to you."

"Do you mean that?" I said, grinning in the dark.

Mum nodded. "You're both clever and you're both creative and just because Crystal hasn't taken up her place at university doesn't mean she won't do well for herself."

"So does that mean I don't have to leave Star Makers?" I said, hardly able to believe what I was hearing. "Are you going to ring Mrs. Raja?"

"Hang on!" said Mum, shaking her head.

"I'm not going to decide just like that. Mrs. Raja is a fantastic tutor, one of the best. We'll talk about it in the morning when I've had a proper chance to think things through."

I hardly slept all night. At some point I texted Ellie to say *Wedding okay but crisis not over yet.* I suppose I must've fallen asleep in the end, because I had a terrible nightmare that I was onstage acting my part in *The Phantom Face* when suddenly I realized I was stark naked in front of the entire audience *and* Adam. I woke up, my heart racing, and lay there in a state of terror until the morning.

Mum came in quite early. She drew my curtains and sat on my bed. She had such a serious look on her face I felt like crawling under the covers before she'd even said anything.

"I've had a long chat with Dad," she said in the end. "You know, about everything..." I nodded, hardly able to breathe. "He thinks it's very important that I let you follow your dreams and I think he's probably right."

"Does that mean...?" I started.

"It means I'm going to come and see you in your show and then afterwards I'll have a proper chat with Mandy. If she thinks you've got real potential, we'll leave the tutoring for a bit and let you concentrate on your acting."

"Are you joking me, Mum?"

"No, Sam." She ruffled my hair. "I'm not joking you. I know you've only got a small part, but I still want to see you do the best you can."

It didn't seem the right moment to tell her I actually had the biggest part in the show, so I threw my arms round her instead and gave her a massive hug.

"You won't regret this," I laughed, jumping out of bed. "You wait until Saturday. You won't believe your eyes!"

* * *

 289

I was desperate to speak to Ellie on Monday. "What happened?" she cried when she saw me. "In your first text you said it had all gone wrong and then later on you said it was kind of okay."

"Well it did all go wrong to start with, but then Tyler sang this amazing song called 'Precious Girl', and then Mum and Crystal sort of made up, and then Mum decided that I could carry on at Star Makers, but only if I do a brilliant performance on Saturday."

"No pressure then," said Polly.

"But you *will* be brilliant," said Phoebe. "You're so good at acting and you've got such a good part and you never get nervous, do you, Sam?"

"Talking of good parts," said Ellie, "does your mum know yet – about you being Laura?"

I shook my head. "She doesn't know and I *am* nervous. More nervous than I've ever been in my life – especially after I was so rubbish at the dress rehearsal. If I mess up again, it'll be goodbye Star Makers, hello Mrs. Raja!"

When we got to drama on Saturday, Sandeep was waiting for us by the door, looking frantic.

"You haven't seen the CD, have you?" he said.

"Do you mean the eerie music CD?" said Polly.

He nodded. "I thought I left it in the CD player with all the other equipment, but it's gone."

"What did Mandy say?" said Ellie. "She always goes mad when I lose my script."

"I haven't told her. I don't dare. Not after all the work Julian put into the sound effects. I mean the first show is in seven hours time and Julian is miles away on another job and I don't know what I'm going to do."

We got changed as fast as we could and ran

back out to help. Phoebe and Polly kept Mandy distracted while the rest of us hunted around for the missing CD. Monty B arrived and made a big show of searching with his giant magnifying glass until Neesha got fed up and snatched it away.

"I'll still find it," said Monty B. "I am a trained detective after all."

Neesha snorted. "Oh my God, yeah, if you find it I swear I'll kiss your feet."

Luckily for her, right at that second Mrs. Beagle came in carrying the CD.

"Does this belong to you?" she said. "I found it in my office and I'm quite certain it's not mine." I thought Sandeep was going to kiss *her* feet for a minute, but he just kissed the CD, thanked her about a million times and then collapsed down on a chair in relief.

"What are you sitting down for?" said Mandy, coming over. "Don't you realize how much there is left to do?"

The rest of the day flew by. We practised a few bits that needed the most work and then spent quite a bit of time helping Mandy with the set. Julian usually does it, but since he wasn't around we all pitched in to get it sorted in time. We had to make the stage look very old-fashioned. Mandy had brought these heavy velvet curtains to hang, and a fake log-fire. It took ages to get the curtains right, and then we had to set out the chairs in the hall and sort out all the sound equipment.

By the time we finished there was only twenty minutes or so until the audience were due to arrive. We were just about to go backstage when Arthur walked in.

"Hello, fellow actors," he boomed. My mouth dropped open and Ellie burst out laughing, trying to hide behind me so he wouldn't see.

"What's happened to your hair, Arthur?" said Mandy, her eyes so big they practically filled her entire face.

"I've had some of those hair extensions," he said. "They're all the rage, you know! That's what I've been trying to talk to you about. I wanted your advice, you see, about the best place to have them done, but luckily one of my parishioners at the church pointed me in the right direction."

I looked round at Ellie, who was still trying to hide behind me. All those times Arthur had come in looking for Mandy and all he'd wanted was advice about her hair extensions!

"Oh," said Mandy. She bit her lip. "They're very...um...long."

"Thank you, my dear, and I just wanted to wish you well for your performance."

He strode out and Mandy literally collapsed laughing. "I am so sorry," she gasped, clutching her stomach. "I know I shouldn't laugh but that's just the funniest thing I've ever seen in my life. I mean, Arthur with hair extensions." She wiped her eyes and took a deep breath, but then she started laughing all over again. "Come on, guys," she managed in the end. "It's time to get ready. I want you to wait backstage now until I give you the signal to come on."

We all trooped into the room behind the stage, laughing and talking about Arthur.

"I am *so* nervous," I said to Ellie. "I mean what if my mum thinks I'm just okay?"

"She won't. You'll be so good you'll probably win an Oscar," she said, grinning. "Good luck with the lights and sound by the way," she called out to Sandeep as he walked past us. "Break a leg!"

"*What!*" said Sandeep.

Ellie started laughing. "It's just an old saying..." she tried to say, but she was laughing so hard she couldn't get the words out. It was so funny it set me off – and then Phoebe – and before long we were all on the floor in hysterics.

"The hall's packed!" said Mandy, coming in.

She stopped dead, looking at us. "For goodness' sake! Not you lot as well! Come on, get up…it's time to go on."

We squashed into the wings, waiting for the lights to go down. I took the deepest breath I could manage and focused all my energy on giving the best performance of my life. Maybe one day I would win an Oscar, but right now the only thing that mattered was convincing Mum that I was deadly serious about being an actress.

The second I walked onstage I stopped being Sam and as if by magic I became Laura: a young, curious girl staying at an ancient castle with her family. The show begins with all of us onstage with the image of the phantom girl projected onto the screen behind us. The eerie music plays out for a minute or so and then Mandy plays the introduction and we sing the opening number.

Sandeep managed to get the image up with

no problems at all, but then, as we were standing there waiting for Julian's music to start, something else began to play out of the speakers.

It wasn't the eerie music at all.

It was Arthur – declaring his undying love for Mrs. Beagle.

21
My Moment in the Spotlight!

I couldn't believe it. After everything I'd been through, Arthur was going to spoil my big moment. Arthur and his stupid crush on Mrs. Beagle was going to ruin my one chance of staying at Star Makers. No one knew what to do. Sandeep was frantically pressing every button in front of him, while Mandy sat rigid on the piano stool with her eyes closed tight. A couple of people in the audience began to titter and laugh as Arthur's voice droned on and on. He'd obviously used Julian's CD to record a message to Mrs. Beagle and then left it on her desk.

"My dearest June," he was saying. "My feelings for you grow stronger by the day. Please, my love, if you feel as strongly for me as I do for you, you must find some way of showing me..."

We all stood there like lemons. The message seemed to go on for ever – it was *June* this, and *June* that. I couldn't actually see my mum – the lights were way too bright – but I knew she was out there, watching everything go wrong. I half-felt like running straight off the stage and hiding away, but I knew that if I did she'd never take me seriously.

My heart started to bang inside my chest. I had to do something – anything – to put things right. Somehow I had to get the audience to think that *June* was the name of the missing girl, instead of April.

The second the recording ended I walked forward, alone, right to the front of the stage. The audience fell silent and all eyes were on me. It was just like the dream I had the other night, but a million times worse. I said a silent prayer and opened my mouth to speak.

"This is the story of a young girl named *June* and the two men who fell in love with her." My voice was shaking but I carried on. "One would win her love; one would be accused of her murder. A story where nothing is quite what it seems and *no one* can be trusted. Ladies and gentlemen... welcome to...THE PHANTOM FACE!"

There was a massive cheer from the audience and Mandy began to play the introduction to the opening number.

The rest of Act One went so well I could hardly believe it. There were no sound effects, obviously, but it just seemed to have an amazing energy, as if everyone was making up for the terrible beginning. Monty B was hilarious and Neesha was fantastic as the butler. Even Sara was good, in an irritating younger sister sort of way.

Mandy came rushing backstage in the interval and grabbed hold of me.

"Sam Lester!" she cried, her eyes shining. "You were a-*mazing*. The way you did that, it was as if we'd rehearsed it for weeks. It was perfect. I could kill Arthur, I really could! I'd like to get hold of his blooming hair extensions and string him up! But I'll never forget you walking forward like that. Honestly, Sam. It was *so* brave and *so* clever."

"Yes, and weren't *we* all clever to keep the June thing going," said Sara. "Well, except for Monty B who kept calling her April."

"I know," said Mandy, "but even that was funny because Detective Biscuit is *supposed* to get everything wrong."

Monty B grinned. "It's amazing how clever I can be when I'm not even trying. It's a real gift."

"She said *funny*, not clever," said Adam. "But seriously, Sam, you really did save the day."

"Oh, it was no big deal," I said, grinning like an idiot. But of course it was a big deal – the biggest!

Act Two was even better than Act One, and

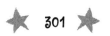

when I came on for my bow I swear I got the biggest cheer. It was the most incredible feeling – I could've easily stood there all night. I'd done the performance of my life and Mum had been there to see it.

"I'm *so* pleased we get to do it all again tomorrow night," I said when we finally got backstage. "I could perform it a million times and I'd never get bored."

"Yeah, me too," said Sandeep, "except *next time* I'm going to check the CDs *before* I play them. I don't think I could take another shock like that. You were really amazing, Sam. How did you know what to say?"

I shrugged, grinning. "I don't know really, it just came out of my mouth."

"Ellie was right," said Phoebe. "You really do deserve an Oscar."

I looked over at Ellie. She was staring off into the distance with a weird expression on her face.

"What's the matter?" I said. "You look as if you've seen a ghost!"

Ellie sighed. "It wasn't a ghost. It was just that boy in the second row. Did you see him? He was so cute. His name's Ollie, apparently, and he's a friend of Neesha."

I rolled my eyes. "Maybe I should warn him not to lend you any clothes!"

"I'm not going to make a habit of freezing my boyfriend's sweatshirts, you know."

"Yeah, well, just so long as you remember, it's Friends First."

"Always!" said Ellie. "And that goes for you too!"

I glanced across at Adam. I still fancied him and I still thought he was drop-dead gorgeous, but my friendship with Ellie was way more important.

"Always!" I said, and gave her the biggest hug.

When I went back out to the hall, Dad and

Aunty Mags were waiting for me with Crystal. I looked around for Mum and saw she was over by the piano, talking to Mandy.

"Here she comes," said Crystal. "The star of the show! How did I ever end up with such a talented little sister?"

"Takes after me of course," joked Dad. "But seriously, Sam, you were fantastic – especially right at the beginning when that recording was playing out." He raised his eyebrow, smiling. He'd obviously twigged it was a mistake.

"Long story!" I said, laughing. "But I'm not going into it now. I've got to go over and see what Mum and Mandy are talking about."

They stopped talking as soon as they saw me coming towards them. It was impossible to tell from Mum's face what she was thinking, but Mandy was grinning from ear to ear.

"I've just been telling your mum how proud she should be," said Mandy. "I still can't get over what you did. You'd maybe expect an experienced actress to react so quickly in a situation like that, but not a twelve year old."

"Almost thirteen," I said, thrilled that Mandy had said something so nice – and in front of Mum.

"Yes, well, twelve or thirteen, it was extraordinary."

"I'll tell you what else is extraordinary," said Mum, with a twinkle in her eye. "The fact that you had so many lines. That has to be the *biggest* small part in the history of the theatre. Anyway, Mandy's just been telling me all about her plans for next term's show."

"Does that mean you're going to let me carry on?" I squealed.

"Of course I am," said Mum. "How could I stop you after that performance? Honestly, it was so good I've told Dad we're coming to watch you again tomorrow night."

I literally threw my arms round her neck, saying "Thank you" over and over. "I'll work so hard, you won't believe it. I'll get As in all my subjects. I'll be top at *everything*!"

"And modest too," said Mandy, laughing.

The next day, Crystal, Tyler, Aunty Mags and Riley all came round to ours for Sunday lunch. Dad opened a bottle of champagne and Mum made Crystal's favourite meal. It was a bit weird and awkward to start with; Tyler looked horribly uncomfortable, and Crystal was still a bit funny around Mum. But then, after lunch, Dad got his Stevie and the Stingrays scrapbooks out and he went through all his cuttings with Tyler. He told Tyler loads of great stories about when he first started out with the band and they even arranged to have some sort of jamming session with their guitars.

Mum and Crystal sat in the kitchen and they talked and talked. About *Crystal's Crystals* and Sophia Malone's wedding and how weird it was that they'd both ended up there – like it was fate or something. They've always been like that – either the best of friends or at each other's throats, arguing.

I escaped into the garden with Aunty Mags and Riley. She showed me all the tricks he'd learned at his first obedience classes. He could sit and lie and walk right next to your heels.

"Isn't he good?" said Aunty Mags. "Except he's still a terrible chewer."

"Don't remind me!" I laughed, thinking about Adam and my ruined bra and that day at drama. "I certainly won't be leaving my underwear on the floor when he's around."

Just before Crystal and Tyler had to go, Crystal said she had an important announcement to make. I saw Mum give Dad a quick look. She probably thought Crystal was going to say she was having a baby or something.

"Tyler and I have decided to wait for a year before we get married – and it's not just because the band's doing so well," she went on before Mum could say anything. "It's also because I'm going to be far too busy over the next few months myself."

"Far too busy doing what exactly?" said Mum, frowning.

"Erm...working with you, of course!" She stopped for a second, grinning. "I mean, now that we're going to be business partners."

"*Business partners?*" said Mum weakly. "Me and you?"

"Come on, Mum, you said yourself that you'd like to sell some of my candleholders in the shop. Well, just think how much we could achieve if we worked together. *Crystal's Crystals* and *Everything's Rosy*. How could it fail?"

Mum went rosy then. I don't know if it was the champagne or the fact that Crystal was back and they were friends again. But whatever the reason, it was brilliant.

"This calls for a song," cried Dad, grabbing his guitar.

"Crystal and Sam…my two special girls,
My two little angels, more precious than pearls.
More precious than pearls with their shiny blonde curls…
Crystal and Sam…my two special girls."

He strummed away, making up more and more verses as he went along, until we were all joining in – even Tyler and Mum. We had "Rosy my wife, she's simply my life…" and "Tyler's band, the best in the land…" and "Aunty Mags and Riley, they make me feel so smiley…"

I couldn't stop smiling either. It was easily the best weekend of my life. Mum and Crystal going into business together, Dad playing the guitar again, and – most important of all – my performance at Star Makers. I'd had my special moment in the spotlight and I couldn't *wait* to go back for more.

Hi guys,

I grew up dreaming about being on the stage. I joined a drama club and spent every spare moment singing and dancing — convinced I was going to be a star.

But at secondary school I began to feel shy about performing. I lost a lot of confidence and for the first time I wasn't sure if my dream to be on stage would come true.

Years later I started up my own drama club, Full Circle. I guess it was a way of keeping my dream alive. I found that running a drama club was as brilliant as performing myself — all the same nerves and excitement!

One day I started to scribble down some ideas for a book about a group of characters who join a drama club. I called it Star Makers. There was Phoebe who was very shy but could sing like an angel and Polly who just wanted everything to stay the same, Sam the big show-off who was desperate to be a serious actress, and Monty B who liked to clown around. I'd created a special place where everyone is different but everyone has their moment to shine.

This is Sam's story. Sam has always been loud and sure of herself — on the outside — but on the inside she's not feeling quite as confident as usual. Some help from her friends and a special performace at Star Makers soon have her smiling again.

I still have BIG dreams — but these days they're much more about writing than about singing and dancing.

Dreams are so important...I hope all of yours come true!

Anne-Marie x

www.annemarieconway.com

ISBN: 9781409516514

Why won't Phoebe's annoying neighbour, Monty B, leave her alone? Can she get her dippy dad and over-worked mum back together again? Will class mean-girl, Polly Carter, just get off her case for once? And most important of all – will she overcome her stage fright in time to sing her musical solo?

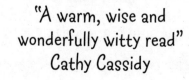

"A warm, wise and wonderfully witty read"
Cathy Cassidy

Why has Polly's mum left her to go and
live in Spain? When will her new stepmum
stop trying to be so nice all the time? What
happens when she ignores Dad and goes on
the friend2friend website? And, most
importantly, can she learn her lines in time for
Star Makers' fab new production?

A warm-hearted story about the triumphs
and traumas at the Star Makers Drama Club
— a special place where everyone has
their moment to shine!

Meet Chloe and her friends —
they all dream of becoming stars and they're
working hard to make it happen at...

Fame School

by Cindy Jefferies

REACH FOR THE STARS   9780746061176
Chloe loves to sing and dreams of becoming a
pop star. But will she win a place at Fame School?

RISING STAR   9780746061183
Chloe is desperate to perform in the Rising Stars
concert, but will her voice be strong enough?

SECRET AMBITION   9780746061206
Model twins Pop 'n' Lolly have always done everything
together. But one of them has a secret ambition.

RIVALS!   9780746061190
Danny's drumming talents are in demand, but his
jealous rival is out to cause trouble.

TARA'S TRIUMPH 9780746068359

Tara wants to produce a charity CD with her friends, but will it be more trouble than she bargained for?

LUCKY BREAK 9780746068366

Marmalade is always showing off, but when a new boy starts looking up to him, he takes things a step too far.

SOLO STAR 9780746073032

Chloe is thrilled to be picked for the Rising Stars concert, but can she learn how to sing with a band?

CHRISTMAS STARS 9780746077429

Can Chloe and her friends impress their favourite teacher with a surprise Christmas concert performance?

POP DIVA 9780746073049

Pop 'n' Lolly have won a recording contract, but will Pop work hard enough to make their single a success?

BATTLE OF THE BANDS 9780746078839

Does Chloe's band still stand a chance of winning the International Battle of the Bands after disaster strikes?

STAR MAKER 9780746097151

Tara's band is set to play a massive charity gig on TV! But will it all go wrong when their drummer falls ill?

DANCING STAR 9780746097168

Marmalade has been picked to dance in a pop video, but will his new-found creative flair impress his friends?

TOTALLY LUCY
by Kelly McKain

Meet Lucy — a wannabe fashion designer and stand-up babe whose life is full of best-friend dilemmas and teacher troubles...

Makeover Magic
9780746066898

When a geeky new girl starts at school, style queen Lucy comes up with a fab Makeover Plan to help her fit in.

Fantasy Fashion
9780746066904

Lucy's fave mag is running a comp to design a fantasy fashion outfit and Lucy is determined to win first prize!

Boy Band Blues
9780746066911

Lucy is mega-excited to be styling a boy band for a Battle of the Bands competition — it's just a shame lead singer Wayne is such a big-head!

Star Struck
9780746070611

Lucy's won a part as a film extra and decides she must get her fab design skills noticed on screen — but will the director appreciate her original efforts?

Picture Perfect

9780746070628

Lucy decides to throw a surprise party for
Tilda's birthday – but will crossed wires wreck
their friendship?

Style School

9780746070635

Lucy sets up a Style School in the loos, but what will
happen when the School Uniform Police finds out?

Summer Stars

9780746080177

The girls are thrilled to be going on holiday together,
especially as their fave mag is holding a dance
competition in the same town!

catwalk crazy

9780746080184

Lucy is putting on a charity show but someone is
sabotaging her efforts. Can she track down the culprit
and win back her audience before it's too late?

Planet Fashion

9780746080191

Tilda's bedroom is a design disaster, until Lucy and
Jules give it an eco-friendly makeover. Maybe their
project will win them a feature on Tilda's fave
TV show, *Go Green*!

Best Friends Forever

9780746080207

Lucy transforms the boring school disco ino a
super-stylish High School Prom. But will she find the
right boy to make her big red-carpet entrance with?

For more Fabulous Fiction, check out
www.fiction.usborne.com